# Mine

## A. N. Senerella

**Inkitt**

**This book is published by Inkitt – Join now to read and discover free upcoming bestsellers!**

# Dedication

To Tiffany McGuire. You believed in me before anyone else did, and you gave me a friend when I needed one. I'll never be able to tell you how thankful I am for your inspiration and kindness when I needed it.

To Scott Newell. Sorry I wrote this during your class instead of taking notes for two years. You're an amazing teacher, and one hell of a friend. I know I can go to your class when I need a break or someone to talk to. Thanks for putting up with me for what's almost been three years now.

To Mary Anderson. You were my first English teacher in the first school I ever truly loved, then my Creative Writing Two teacher, and you kept things fun and interesting for all of us. Thank you for helping me push my limits as a writer.

To Reneé Motter. My first Creative Writing teacher, you helped me form new styles and ways of thinking. Your class was excellent and I wish I could take it again.

I don't feel like teachers get the credit they deserve, but these four in particular impacted me in ways that will change the rest of my life, and this was the least I could say for them. I didn't like who I was when I met these people, and I had no faith in my abilities. Each of them helped me fix that, one day and one way at a time.

Oh, and also to Sam McCracken, because while I was typing up this page for the hundredth time, she said, "Oh, and to me, just for fun, *lol*". You helped motivate me to finish this book when I thought I couldn't do it. Thanks.

I love you all.

# Chapter 1

Just like any high school, mine was always buzzing with gossip and rumors. Not that I paid much attention to them. If I heard them, I'd listen, but I never gave them much credibility because I'd played the game Telephone as a kid and I knew how badly things got distorted when passed from person to person. Especially when there was one kid that wanted to stir things up a little. Today was different though. Rather than gossip, everyone was talking about some new guy and setting up competitions to see who could get his phone number first. I remembered four months ago when the same thing had happened with Franklin, the poor guy. He was still dating one of the lowest lowlifes on the planet, and he didn't seem to care that she was cheating on him with roughly five other guys. Some guys were just desperate, I guess.

My day already sucked. My penguin pendant—the one I'd worn around my neck since I was in elementary school because of my love for penguins—had disappeared. I'd woken up ten minutes late and had to get a ride with Sierra and even though I loved her—she *was* one of my best friends after all—she was definitely not someone I wanted to be near in the morning. She was one of those people who woke up in the morning as if she was going to Disneyland or something. I, on the other hand, was the kind of person you had to roll out of bed and, by doing so, you'd be at risk of being beaten for waking me up. Her perkiness was normally kind of nice, but in the morning it made me want to choke her.

The night before, my hair had dried weird, so it was falling in tangled waves halfway down my back instead of being in a messy bun where it was normally stored. I hadn't even tried to yank a brush through the tangled mess, but it still looked kind of neat; windblown, almost. Except, the way less hot version of whatever image that sends through your mind.

Now I was at my locker, glaring at it because my combination wasn't working. Once a month or so this would happen, causing me to have to go get a janitor to open it for me because it was jammed for no reason whatsoever. Lucky me.

I sighed sharply in anger at the locker and kicked the bottom of it, hard. Luckily, all my shoes had steel toes so it didn't hurt me, but it clearly messed up the locker a little bit. Not enough for anyone to notice it, but enough that I had a small panic attack from seeing it. Something clicked when I kicked it, and I thoughtfully pulled on the latch, swinging the locker open easily. "Finally," I muttered victoriously. After tossing my books in without bothering to make them tidy, I turned around to start walking and ran straight into the chest of some guy. I gasped sharply, apologizing under my breath.

"You looked like you were having trouble."

"I'm fine." Ugh. I didn't want to start a conversation; I wanted to get to my first class and get it over with so that I could just move on with my day and go enjoy my weekend. "Please move." I sighed when we did the thing where you kind of step in the way, mirroring the other person, so neither of you can pass.

He stepped to the left with a lengthy stride to let me pass.

I walked around him quickly, but something caught the handle of my backpack and almost sent me flying backward from the sudden resistance to my gait.

"How've you been, Anika?"

I glared up at the boy, looking at his face for the first time, feeling as though my stomach had sunk through my feet. Oh. Great. It was Brady. This moron was the most irritating person I'd ever known in my life and was one of the more 'popular' guys in the school. All the more reason to dislike him, in my opinion. "I'd be better if you would let go of my backpack."

He snorted.

I struggled, then sighed. "You know what? I don't have time for this crap." I slipped my arms out of the backpack and pulled my phone out of my pocket, texting Sierra that I needed to borrow some paper and pens for first period because someone had decided to play keep-away during passing period. Once I reached my Astronomy class, I assumed my regular seat in the back left corner of the room at the small cluster of desks that were completely uninhabited except for me. The bell rang, and there was no sign of Sierra. I groaned mentally. This was going to be miserable. Maybe the teacher would let me borrow a pencil.

Most people would probably not leave their backpack with someone like Brady, but the truth was that when I was angry, I truly didn't care about anything. Someone could come up to me and grab my leg and I would probably just saw it off to get away from them before I slowed down and asked them to let go of it. Therefore, I no longer had a backpack.

Eh. It would probably make its way back to me eventually.

As always, Mr. Shrem started class late. When he rushed in, I shook my head, smiling. He was my favorite teacher. "Sorry, students. There's a new student in the school, and he was having a hard time finding the room."

*Sure, Shrem,* I scoffed mentally, smiling.

"This is Foster Woods. He's an incoming junior from Alaska, I believe." Shrem motioned vaguely to the boy standing in front of the chalkboard. The first thing I noticed was that he was *huge*. Most of the guys at this school were between five ten and six two, but this guy looked like he was seven foot twelve or something from the way he towered over Mr. Shrem. He had black hair and a slight arrogance in his stance that bothered me for whatever reason. The second thing I noticed was that his eyes were locked on me. Which, in all likeliness, was probably what I should've noticed first, but I wasn't one for eye contact. And finally, the last thing I noticed? *He had my backpack.*

How the hell? Brady had it last time I checked. Ugh. New to the school and already buddied up with the village idiot. Great choice. Whatever. As long as I got my backpack back, I didn't really care that he had it.

His gaze was intense and I shifted a little bit, thinking that if he saw me looking at him, he would look away from me. Unfortunately, that wasn't the case. Foster's eyes were locked dead on mine, and he didn't show signs of looking away. I couldn't tell what color they were from here, but I assumed they were blue. Black-haired boys with blue eyes were always the bad boys in this school, and he definitely had the "bite me" vibe. There was something vaguely familiar about him, but I couldn't put my finger on it.

Shrem cleared his throat awkwardly. I loved how awkward he was. "Um… Foster, care to share a few things about yourself?"

Foster was still looking at me. "I'm seventeen, I'm a junior, and I'm not available. I say that because I've been asked several times and it's getting rather bothersome."

At least six girls groaned in defeat. I laughed, rolling my eyes and looking away from Foster. There were slight chills touching my spine; he had been addressing the class, but I had felt like he was talking only to me when he spoke. Stupid, I know, but the eye contact made me feel like it was a little more directed than it actually was. Maybe that was just what eye contact did, though.

Shrem laughed a little. "Alright. You can take a seat wherever you like. Anika's entire table group is open, so feel free to go sit over there."

Why? Why would he do that? No. Come on, Shrem. Why?

Foster walked over to my table group and took the seat diagonal to mine, facing me but not directly in front of me. He didn't say anything but tossed my backpack carefully over the tables so that it fell into the seat next to me.

Surprise flashed through my body for a moment before I nodded to him to say thanks.

He nodded back.

I reached into my bag and pulled out my Astronomy notebook, looking down at my notes and flipping through them while Mr. Shrem explained something I probably wasn't interested in hearing about. When he set a test down in front of me, I almost jumped in surprise. I looked at him for an answer, but he just laughed and shook his head. The test stared up at me evilly. I hated those things with their imaginary numbers and hard to understand words that I wasn't sure actually existed. *Penumbra.* Who the hell knew what that was? It's not like I was a scientist.

I glanced up, and Foster was looking at me like he was expecting something. It was tempting to just blurt out "What?" but he had been nice enough to give me my backpack, so I decided to ignore it and just turn back to my test. After ten minutes, I was pretty sure he was still watching me. I could feel his eyes on me, and I did my best not to look at him. His eyes were burning holes into me; I could feel it. Finally, I couldn't take it anymore. "Stop. Looking. At. Me," I quietly growled between my teeth to the boy less than three feet from me. What was his problem? Was he trying to cheat on the test or something? Poor choice on his part; I didn't know any of the material either. *Ha, sucks to be you if you're trying to cheat.* I felt slightly victorious. Did that count as a victory?

Foster didn't reply.

The rest of the class continued like that. I could just *feel* him watching me. The whole time. It was kind of creepy. So, when the bell rang, I almost bolted out of the classroom. Just outside of the Astronomy room, though, someone grabbed my backpack and yanked hard. This time, I flew backward into someone. When I spun around, I punched blindly.

Mitchell doubled over instantly and my eyes widened.

"Oops," I said awkwardly.

He groaned. "If I didn't love you, I would hate you right now."

It was all suddenly very funny to me. I started laughing at my other best friend as he pretended like he had been shot or something. To be fair, I probably hit him pretty hard. So what? I was irritated and creeped out. Really it was his fault. Mitchell glared up at me from his bent position and I grinned at him. "Well, you shouldn't have grabbed my bag like that. Brady did it earlier and it pissed me off pretty bad."

He straightened himself up and sighed. "I changed my mind. I hate you."

I snorted. "Nah. You love me."

He glared again and I blew him a kiss dramatically. "Next time, I'm gonna hit you back."

"I'd like to see you try."

"Oh yeah?"

"Yeah. Come at me, Ross." We play-fought all the time, and I always called him by his last name when we did. I raised my fists teasingly and Mitchell brought his fist backward so that he could do his lame punch thing; basically, he would pretend to actually punch me pretty hard, but his hand would slow down dramatically at the last second and barely tap my shoulder. I lightly kicked his shin and laughed, and he started to do his stupid habitual punch, but suddenly someone had him by the elbow.

I stared at Foster.

The look on Foster's face… Well, have you ever heard the phrase: "If looks could kill?" This one could wipe out a country.

Mitchell turned around in confusion and Foster roughly pushed him away, against the locker.

"What the hell?" I yelped, grabbing onto Mitchell's other arm and trying to pull him away.

Mitchell looked terrified. He was only five foot nine, just two inches taller than I was, and he was not exactly a body builder. In fact, he was captain of the chess club, if that hints at all toward his body type.

Foster looked dead into Mitchell's eyes, his arm like a bar across the smaller boy's chest to keep him against the locker. "What were you doing?"

I glared angrily and shoved Foster's arm. "Let go of him!" I ordered.

His eyes shifted toward me in consideration, their dark blackish-brown depths looking down into my blue ones. "He was going to hit you." As if that explained it! Why the hell was he attacking Mitchell? It's not like he had done anything to him!

"No, he wasn't. That's just some stupid game we play."

"It's definitely stupid," he agreed, coldly.

"You know what else it is? None of your business. Let go of Mitchell." Foster removed his arm from Mitchell's chest and I yanked him toward me suddenly, away from his attacker. I was certain that my evil eye could match Foster's, and his look of

6

suppressed anger was now just an acidic glare. I didn't look away from him and instead met his glare with my own. We stayed like that for a while before Mitchell tugged on my arm gently, pulling my attention away from Foster.

"Anika, we have to go now," Mitchell muttered into my ear. "You're causing a scene."

"*He's* causing the scene," I hissed.

He was right, though. There were roughly ten people just staring at me and Foster, waiting to see what would happen. Finally, I tore my gaze away from Foster and grabbed Mitchell's hand, towing him away from the hallway.

My phone buzzed, and I ignored it. It was probably just Sierra apologizing for not bringing me paper or a pencil. This boy was weird. He'd attacked Mitchell, and he'd gotten my backpack out of nowhere and returned it to me. I sat down on my seat in the choir with my friend and grimaced, looking at him apologetically. "Are you okay?"

Mitchell rubbed his chest lightly. "That hurt," he grumbled.

"I can imagine it did."

"What was that all about, anyway?"

"As if I know."

He sighed and my phone buzzed yet again. Really not the best time, Sierra.

"Are you okay?" I repeated, glancing over the rest of his visible skin for any injuries. "You don't look too beat up, so I guess you can't be too bad." His face flushed red as I looked him over and I laughed. "You're such a loser. I love you."

"Losers are better anyway."

I grinned. My phone buzzed again.

For the love of—

I pulled out my phone and looked at the messages.

**is he a friend of yours?**

**or are you two dating?**

**either way, if I see him put his hands on you in any way i'll break off his arms.**

I stared at the unknown number. Putting two and two together, I realized it could be Foster. Three things about this bothered me. One: he was threatening Mitchell. Two: the entire line of questioning and his statement were creepy. And three: how in the *hell* had he gotten my phone number? My thumbs flew across the screen as I replied.

**Is this Foster?**

**yes.**

The reply came so quickly that I was certain he had been waiting for my reply. I felt like I was going to be sick. There was something wrong with this guy.

**How did you get my phone number...? You've been at this school less than a day.**

**brady gave it to me.**

Oh. Wonderful. Just great. Note to self: beat the crap out of Brady next time I see him. It didn't surprise me that *he* had my number because I'd been paired up with him multiple times on school projects. Not that he had remembered to actually help me on almost any of them. Clearly he remembered enough to have my phone number, though. Boys were so infuriating.

**Don't touch Mitchell again, or else.**

**is that a threat?;)**

**Yes. Do. Not. Touch him.**

**this is backward. your the one thats meant to be listening to me, not the other way around.**

**Excuse me? I don't know you, and even if I did you can't order me around.**

**you do. you just don't realize it yet**

Chills shot through my entire body. This was so weird. What could he possibly want? *You do know me, you just don't realize it yet.* What did that even mean? I shoved my phone into my pocket, not bothering to reply, and looked at Mitchell. I guess I looked pretty shaken because concern shot across his face instantly.

"You okay?"

"He has my phone number now."

"Who?"

"Foster."

"Who's Foster?" Mitchell's face was blank and his eyebrows pushed together uncertainly. For a genius, he could be really thick sometimes.

"The guy that just handed your ass to you on a silver platter."

"Report him for harassment or something, then."

"And say what? 'A boy is texting me?' I'll just block his number or something. He's a creep." I sighed as the choir instructor walked into the room. "We'll talk about this during lunch when Sierra's there for me to bounce ideas off of."

"Alright, I guess."

He didn't sound too convinced, but I didn't really care if he believed me. I was seriously creeped out.

What was wrong with this guy?

# Chapter 2

"What the hell is your problem, Anika?"

I raised my eyebrow at Brady. "Nice to see you too."

"No, don't give me that. Why'd you set your boyfriend on me because *you* left your backpack with me? It's not my fault you left. If you think you can seriously just have some guy intimidate me into doing what you want, you're wrong, got it?"

Now I was confused. "I didn't do anything like that." Slowly, a chill spread through my body as I suddenly I realized who he was talking about.

"Why are you so pale?"

"That's Foster." I rubbed my temples, massaging as though I could rid myself of this problem simply by rubbing my head. "He's weird, and he's been beating the hell out of anyone who goes near him. Or... near me I guess. Either way, he's getting on my nerves and needs to stay away from me."

Brady looked at me thoughtfully.

"What?"

"So he's just a stalker then?"

"That's not what I said." But yes, he certainly seemed that way at the moment.

Brady took a seat across from me.

"What in the world are you doing?"

"I'm sitting."

"Really? I thought you were doing ballet." I rolled my eyes. "Why are you sitting here?"

"Well, someone's gotta keep him away from you."

"Why are you trying to help me?"

"I want to."

I leaned forward so my forehead hit the table. The entire male population was dedicated to driving me completely insane today, I was certain of it. First, some random guy I'd never met claimed that I did, in fact, know him, and now, Brady was sitting with me at lunch after basically ignoring me for however many years. What the hell had happened overnight to make everything go crazy?

"Aw, did you hurt yourself? I could kiss that better if you want."

"Screw you."

"Well, if you insist. I mean, I don't have any other plans, so…"

I lifted my head just a little bit and let it fall against the table again. Maybe if I just hit my head against something hard enough, I could forget that today was happening and wake up in, like, two years or something. That sounded great. A two-year nap. I hadn't realized how tired I was until right now. Maybe that's what it was; maybe the world wasn't going insane, and it was just me imagining things. If my mind was doing this to me, though, that meant I was subconsciously masochistic, because dealing with these people was starting to become physically painful.

"I wasn't kidding," Brady informed me seriously.

"Have you ever wanted to beat the stupid out of someone?"

"Yes, why?"

"Because that's all I can think about right now."

"Um…" Sierra's voice came questioningly as she approached the table and noticed our intruder.

"I don't know, so don't ask me," I groaned.

I felt her sit next to me on the bench, and I felt Mitchell sit on my other side. I continued hitting my head on the table; enough to make a noise and express my frustration, but not hard enough to actually hurt me. Mitchell rubbed my shoulder gently and my phone buzzed. His hand was rubbing circles on my back when I read the text and I paled instantly as I read it.

**didn't i tell you what would happen if i saw that creep touch you?**

I sat up instantly and looked around for Foster. Mitchell retracted his arm, and Brady looked confused. Sierra didn't know a thing about what was going on, so she didn't question it at all until she saw the looks on the other two's faces. "He's watching me. This weirdo is watching me." My lips were numb and my tone was flat.

Brady's eyebrows pushed together. "He is?"

"Yes."

Suddenly, Brady leaned across the table. I reacted just in time to move my face enough that he kissed my cheek rather than whatever he'd been aiming for. I jolted in surprise and fell backward in my attempt to scoot away from him as quickly as possible. My back was flat against the ground and my calves were on the seat where my butt had been previously. I'd hit my head when I fell and I groaned. "What is going on with the world?"

Sierra squeaked in alarm and immediately grabbed one of my arms, dragging me back up into the chair to the best of her ability. Then again, she was so tiny that she didn't actually *have* much ability, so I almost didn't move at all, aside from my arm reacting to Sierra's pulling. I gripped her forearm and pulled myself up into the chair, glaring at Brady immediately upon my return.

Brady looked surprised and a little bit offended. "Kissing me appalls you that much?"

"Why did you do that?"

"I'm offended that you rejected me so severely."

"Why did you do that?" I repeated, more irritably.

"I mean, I know you're not exactly my type of girl or anything, but I'm still pretty much the hottest guy living, let alone going to this school. I doubt anyone better's gonna try to kiss you, so it might as well be me."

This was going nowhere fast. He had ignored my question to indulge in his own meaningless rant about how great he thought he was. I stood up, looking down at them. "Well, that's enough crazy for me today," I announced when I had gotten to my feet. "I'm done. I'm going home, and I'm transferring schools because this one has clearly launched itself into some weird Hell designed specifically for me."

"You're skipping again?" Sierra asked, disappointed.

Brady smirked. "Kinda hot that you're breaking the rules."

"You!" I said, jabbing my finger toward Brady. "Stop being weird! Go back to being the moron that didn't notice me, would you? You're pissing me off!" I looked at Mitchell with equal irritation. "You! Learn how to fight, for the love of God!"

"I didn't even do anything!" he protested, with slightly widened eyes.

"And you! Hit the gym or something. You weigh about as much as a sugar cookie and you'll never fight anyone off or physically help someone like that!" I growled at Sierra. When I'd regained control of myself, I glared, made a loud noise of frustration and threw my hands up. "I'm leaving. If one of you wants to come with me, come with me. This does not include you, Brady. You stay away from me. You're creeping me out too, now."

He started to defend himself, or possibly just to reply to my sudden attack, but I spun on my heel and fled the cafeteria as casually as I could, making my way to the door leading outside.

The second I reached the student parking lot, I felt like I was actually going to explode.

Foster was leaning against my car.

Why?

Why was this happening?

Why was *anything* happening at this point?

"Get away from my car, creep," I half sighed as I approached him.

He grinned. "Hi."

"Are you deaf?"

"Someone's grumpy."

*Someone's being stalked by some creepy guy and having a random guy try to kiss her and having her best friend get beaten up.* "My day has not gone well in any sense of the word, and I would appreciate it if you left me alone. In fact, I can think of national tragedies that have gone better than my day has so far, and feel free

13

to ask me why because I have a list." Like Angelina Whatever breaking up with Brad Something, for example. *So what, Anika? Just pay attention to your own life. You aren't the celebrity and you don't know them, so their choices have nothing to do with you.* Okay. Maybe I was a little angrier about that than I should have been. "You creep me out, you somehow managed to get my phone number, and I don't want to deal with any more people today."

He tilted his head. "You're interesting."

"Okay?"

He grinned again. "I like interesting, and I like you."

"You know what I like? Boys that don't stalk me."

"So you have a type, then?"

I felt like slamming my head into a wall repeatedly to simulate what it felt like to talk to him rather than actually talking to him. Either way, I would probably end up with the same headache intensity. "What are you even talking about?"

"What's your type?"

"Of what?"

"Guy."

"What?" My tone was exhausted, and I felt drained by this conversation as it ran around in circles. It was draining my will to live, slowly but surely.

"What kind of guys do you like?"

"If I answer, will you get away from my car so I can leave?"

"I'll consider it."

"I don't like the whole 'wannabe player bad boy' thing. It's just irritating. Guys who beat up other guys for no reason bother me. Guys who stalk me *bother* me. Guys who watch me and wait for me by my car *bother me.*"

"You're a bit hostile."

What could I even reply to that with?

"I want to be friends," he announced.

"There's no way I'm getting rid of you, is there?"

"No."

14

"Why?"

"Because you're interesting, and I want you."

Whoa. Sounding a little horror movie, there. I suddenly felt very uncomfortable being alone with him. A thousand scenarios flashed through my mind, from kidnapping to having the SWAT team randomly swoop down with a net and take him away, and tell me that he was an experimental design they use to find people and scare them into submission. That one seemed more likely. Now I just had to find his deactivation switch. Maybe I could return to my life then. "Not only do I not understand what that means, I don't want to know."

An arm wove itself around my waist and I almost jumped out of my skin as I felt the warmth of someone else against me.

"Hey. Who's this?"

I had never been so thankful for Sierra in my entire life.

"This is Foster."

Sierra offered her hand to him, and he looked at me hesitantly, slowly taking her hand but not looking away from me. She smiled at him. "Hey, you're new right? Then it makes sense that you don't know about her boyfriend. He really wouldn't like it if you were hitting on her, though, and I don't think that's something a good person does."

"Boyfriend." Foster's eyes blazed suddenly.

"Um… yeah," I squeaked. *Lie. Lie fast. Who was the last person you talked to? Just say Mitchell. No, no, say someone you wouldn't mind seeing killed.* "It's… Brady." *Well, I mean, kind of nailed it? I guess?*

Sierra's nails dug into my side in warning. She wanted me to stop talking. I'd just given a name, and this guy was clearly unstable. I had probably just signed Brady's death certificate in cursive. Not that I really liked him that much, but still, I felt a little guilty, and I would probably feel even more guilty when this sociopath murdered him and we all had to watch his body being scooped out of the lake on the news.

"Brady." His eyes blazed darker like pools of black fire.

I was almost actually scared.

If there was anyone in the school with a chance of surviving this intense boy, though, it was probably Brady; that much was true, but Foster was taller by about an inch and built in a very muscular way. Foster's fist flashed out and into the side of my poor car, making a bang loud enough to make me jump. Sierra jumped as well and we watched in horror as Foster stalked toward the school.

Brady was dead. He was so dead.

"So… if Brady survives, how're you gonna explain this?"

"With lots of apologies and money."

"Good plan. You might need to pay the hospital bills."

***

My phone rang at around five p.m., and I answered it cautiously, not sure if I wanted to talk to the person who had flashed up on the caller ID.

"So. How long have we been dating?"

"I needed to lie. You were the most recent person I'd been near. Hey, did Foster kick your ass?"

"No, he didn't. He didn't come anywhere near me, actually. Sierra told me."

"Um… yeah. Sorry. I wasn't trying to get you killed."

He laughed on the other end of the line. "I'm not afraid of that guy."

"Right."

Brady paused thoughtfully. "If we're gonna pretend to date, you should commit to it a little more. Like, not freaking out and nearly falling to your death when I try to kiss you. In fact, you should get really accustomed to me kissing you."

"Whoa, whoa, whoa. I never said we were gonna do that."

"Do you want to deal with him finding out you lied?"

I was in a corner. Both of the options I had appalled me. Death, or pretend to date Brady. Tough call. "Fine," I said reluctantly. "I'm not going to kiss you unless I have to, though. I mean, unless I *really* have to. I've never kissed anyone and I was really having my first kiss be with you."

"You're a kiss virgin?"

"…What?"

"Kiss virgin. You've never been kissed."

"Yeah. So what?"

"Just surprised me, that's all."

I didn't see why. It's not like I was all that social. "Whatever. So, cover story. How long have we been dating?"

"Two months sounds safe."

"Exact day," I sighed impatiently

"November third."

"Okay. Tell me something about you."

"What?"

"I can't claim to be dating you and know nothing about you. So start talking."

"I'm tired."

"It's five."

"Fine, then I'm lazy and don't want to be on the phone anymore." Boys were so frustrating. "Fine," I growled. "Whatever."

"Bye, *babe*," he said in a mockingly flirtatious voice.

I grimaced and heard the click of him hanging up on the other end of the line. As soon as the line went dead, I fell face first onto my bed and just stared into the nothingness of my closed eyes. Today was so weird. What was going on with the world?

And how was I going to get out of it?

# Chapter 3

I didn't even get twenty-four hours before Brady decided that he wanted to bother me again. My phone rang at seven in the morning on Saturday and, being the person I was, I ignored it. It rang five more times before I picked up the phone and threw it across the room, against a wall, and went back to sleep. At ten, I finally got out of bed and walked over to my phone to call him, sifting through the pile of clothes that it had landed on when I'd thrown it. He picked up on the first ring and I sighed. "What were you calling me for, Brady?"

"You're coming to my party tonight, so I need you to look hot."

I didn't reply at first. Me, looking "hot"? That was a physical improbability. "Excuse me?"

"Look, Foster's coming to the party. So if he sees you with me, he might take a hint."

If he was lying, I couldn't tell. On the other hand, he was a very good liar, and I was one of the most oblivious people in the world. "Fine, whatever. I don't own any dresses though, and *you* sure as hell don't get a say in it."

"Do I get a say in it if I pay for it?"

"No. You're not buying me anything."

"Why?"

I hated it when people bought things for me, regardless of how I knew said person. And I was *not* going to owe Brady anything when this was over. I just wanted to get Foster to back off, maybe have a little fun poking the bear in the process, and get out of this with at least the majority of my sanity. "Because you're not. What time is the party?"

"Six."

"When's it over?"

"When everyone has alcohol poisoning."

"I don't drink."

He groaned on the other end of the line. "Oh God, you're gonna be *that* person."

Moron. "I value the law, thank you."

"Okay. Just look hot tonight and I won't bother you."

Horndog. "Get off my phone."

Brady snorted, but he hung up.

Jerk. My phone rang about four seconds later and I answered it. "What do you want, Brady?" I snapped, without bothering to actually look at the caller ID. Bad choice on my part.

"Having relationship problems?"

Foster's voice sent ice down my spine. "No. I'm just a little cranky at the moment."

"Your boyfriend's hosting a party."

"Yeah… and?"

"Are you going?"

"Why?"

"Because if you don't go, there's really no reason for me to go."

I sighed and contemplated my options. If I did go to the party, I'd probably somehow have to prove I was dating Brady in front of Foster. If I didn't, Foster might think I was lying and I wasn't ready to die yet. *Though that might change if I'm forced to put up with these people too long.* Really, there was no winning. So I took a deep breath and forced a happy tone. "Yeah, of course I'm going. He throws parties like this all the time. They're fun." Well, the first two parts were true. I'd never been to his parties, though he threw them a lot, but I imagined they weren't really fun, especially with my social anxiety that tried to choke me when I was in crowds.

"See you then."

He hung up and I groaned, flopping back down on my bed. If I could get out of this, I needed to. I had plans with Mitchell tonight;

there was an extra-large pizza and a list of horror movies waiting for us. *Oh, for the love of God. I forgot Mitchell.* So—because why not?—I started a third phone call. "Mitchell?" I asked when he picked up.

"Yeah?"

"You have to come to a party tonight, and you have to bring Sierra. Please."

"You're going to Brady's party? I thought we had a date with chess and movies."

"I don't have a choice."

He hesitated, but gave in eventually. That was one of the perks of having best friends; they generally had to go along with whatever stupid plans I had. "Alright, I'll tell her."

"Okay. See you there. Come pick me up at five or something, alright?"

"Sure."

"Bye."

"Bye."

I closed my eyes. Hopefully I didn't need to make any more phone calls. What was I going to do about a dress, though? Maybe I didn't need one. There were some cute partyish shirts in my closet somewhere, and I probably had a pair of jeans without a hole in them somewhere. *Ha. Try telling me to be hot. Like that'll happen.* Rolling myself out of bed, I decided that I should probably start looking for an outfit now if there was a chance in hell of me finding one. Even though there were probably metric tons of clothing throughout my house, I'd have to sort through the pile of clothes in my closet to find a decent party shirt, and then I'd probably have to wash it if I did somehow manage to find it in the depths of Narnia.

Wonderful.

\*\*\*

I looked at myself in the mirror. The only pair of jeans I could find without holes in them were black skinny jeans that didn't come as high up on my hips as I would have liked them to. My shirt was pretty simple. I wore just a loose gray crop top with a white tank top on underneath it to avoid showing my stomach. One sleeve was hanging lazily off of my shoulder. Because of the tank top underneath, I didn't really care. Still, I pulled it back up to sit properly on my shoulder and picked a pair of sandals out.

I looked at the black strappy shoes hesitantly, turning them over in my hand a couple of times and watching them glitter faintly. What were the chances of there being vomit or beer on the floor and that I would walk through it? Immediately, I changed my mind and snagged my combat boots. They were comfortable, and they covered my feet.

Finally, I looked at the mess that was my hair. It was falling in messy waves down my back to my waist, and I sighed, pulling it up into my usual messy bun. My makeup was nice; the only thing I enjoyed about dressing up was the portion that involved me doing my makeup. I had eyeliner and smoky gray eyeshadow encircling my blue eyes to make them look lighter in color and larger in size, and I had a little bit of glitter in the inner corners. I had put pale pink lip gloss on, and even a tiny bit of blush. Brady had better be thankful I had gone through this hassle; it was almost three and I had only just finished getting ready for his stupid party. Between the shower and the cleaning my clothes and the drying my hair, I had wasted four and a half hours pretty easily. Now I was just standing in front of my mirror and wishing I didn't have to go to his house.

There was a knock on my bedroom door.

I turned and Mitchell slipped through the door. His eyes widened when he saw me. "Um... wow. Hi, Anika." He blushed a little and averted his eyes. "Your sleeve is down. I can see your bra strap."

"Oh, God. The world is ending because I, a teenager with boobs, am exposing the strap of a bra that no one must know I'm wearing. No one shall know that I own one; it is against the rules that a female should wear these and I should be punished to the full extent of the law." I rolled my eyes at him. "Either calm down or shut up, if you don't mind." I fixed my sleeve and looked him over. He was in a casual shirt and a decent pair of jeans. "You look pretty good. Do you have hair gel in your hair?"

He nodded as his eyes wandered back over to me. Mitchell's hair was indeed spiked with hair gel, a welcome change to the fluffy mess it had been for most of our lives. Not that I didn't like his hair messy; that's how he always wore it, and it was very… Mitchell of him. But change was good once in a while.

I smiled. "It looks good."

Mitchell smiled at me and gestured. "You do too."

"Why are you here so early, though?"

"Sierra said that if I didn't come check on you now, you'd probably give up on trying to get dressed and go back to bed. Then she explained exactly how she would kill me without leaving evidence if I let you miss the party." He grinned. "She's kinda scary, but we gotta love her. Also, forensically, she didn't make any major errors in her explanation so I think she might actually have gotten away with it. I didn't want to take that chance."

I rolled my eyes. "Sierra is a kitten."

He smiled and shook his head. "Whatever. Do you wanna go meet up with her before the party? I was thinking we could go eat something beforehand so you don't get hungry from all the acting you're gonna do tonight."

I nodded. "Makes sense."

We drove to a fast food place after Mitchell texted Sierra. She met us there late, and her look was… surprising.

She had very dark makeup, and I was pretty sure she had tried contouring. Her outfit was mostly black, except for the exposed skin of her lower back and some of her stomach showing through the lacy bottom of the shirt she was wearing. Sierra grinned at me and Mitchell when she walked in and half jogged toward us, stumbling a little in her black sandals. Side note: this is the girl who I thought only owned pink clothes, high heels and light-colored makeup. "Hey! You guys look great. Why does Mitchell look like a porcupine, though?"

He blushed, irritated, and glared at her.

I laughed a little harder than I probably should have. "It's hair gel. I happen to think it looks very nice. You took four years to get here, though, so he and I already ate. Party starts in, like, half an hour, so you can eat in the car if you still want to get something here."

She shook her head. "I'll eat there, I guess. Besides, Mitchell didn't even text me to meet you guys until, like, six minutes ago."

I looked at Mitchell for an answer, raising my eyebrow, but he shrugged it off and I dismissed it as his forgetfulness. Honestly, it wasn't all that uncommon for him to forget to invite Sierra to the things we did; half the time when it was meant to be all three of us, it ended up being just him and me because Sierra never got the memo.

I got into the car with Mitchell. As we pulled up to Brady's house, I was unable to suppress the groan that escaped my lips. The house was practically shaking from how loud the music was, and there were already drunks staggering around in the front yard. This was going to be absolutely miserable. "We have a plan, right?" I asked, turning my head to face Mitchell with a subtle look of desperation.

"Yeah. Rule one?"

"Don't drink anything that we didn't bring ourselves," I recited. We'd formed this plan on the way here, and I held up one of the water bottles Mitchell had brought so as to punctuate my statement.

"Rule two?"

"Don't eat anything."

"Rule three?"

"If either of us says the word 'lemon', we leave the party immediately."

"Okay, that's all of them. Let's go."

I reached to push open my door, but it opened before I had the chance to do it myself. Foster offered his hand and I got out of the car without taking it. He smirked, then his eyes traveled over me slowly. "You look good, Anika," he breathed huskily as he looked me over.

"Lemon," I muttered.

"Excuse me?"

"Nothing. I thought you weren't coming."

"You said you were coming. So I came."

23

I shrugged and walked around him into the house. Truthfully, I didn't want to go into the house yet, especially without Mitchell going in at the same time, but I wanted to escape Foster as quickly as I could, and that meant going inside. Music erupted around me and, as a crowd of people flooded around me, I felt my pulse quicken. There were way too many people for my liking.

My grip tightened on my water bottle and I kept my head down, walking toward where I hoped the back door was.

When I reached it, I went outside and panted lightly. It was hard to breathe in the house, and I'd basically ended up jogging to the back door. I looked warily at the pool. I couldn't swim and the pool was making me a little nervous. There were probably twelve people in the pool, and I could tell none of them could touch the bottom of it. If I couldn't stand up in a pool, I'd drown, end of story.

An arm slipped around my shoulders and I stiffened.

"You like the party so far?" Brady asked. He was yelling directly into my ear but, because of our proximity to the stereos, I could still barely hear him.

"I've been here for, like, three minutes," I yelled back.

He offered me a soda. I looked at the can and hesitated, biting my lip slightly. Mitchell and I had agreed not to drink anything while we were here, and I wasn't exactly in the mood to be drugged and killed and found in the woods a hundred miles from the last place I was seen. Brady waited but when I didn't take it, he looked kind of offended and annoyed. He glared at me and made a point of raising the can to his lips and drinking from it. His hand slipped from my shoulders to my hand and he started pulling me toward the pool.

I put on the brakes immediately, leaning away from him and digging my heels down in an attempt to stop him from dragging me.

"What's wrong with you?"

"I can't... um..." I looked at the pool, then Brady.

He waited briefly as he thought. "You can't swim?"

"No."

Brady sighed and changed direction, pulling me inside and back through the horde of people. When we got to the living room, he pulled me down so I was sitting on the couch next to him and put my water bottle on the table next to me. I turned my body to face him and he smirked at me. "I'm guessing parties aren't exactly your thing, Anika."

"No. I have… problems when it comes to crowds of people. It makes it hard to breathe and I get dizzy."

"Is that why you've never been to any of mine?"

*Well, that and the fact that I just don't like you.* "Yeah."

He nodded and his eyes trailed around me to look at something behind me. Suddenly, Brady yanked me toward him a little roughly and put his lips right next to my ear. "Foster is looking. Either kiss me or pretend to." He pulled back his face and left it mere centimeters from mine, his hand slipping to cup my cheek as he did so. We just stared at each other. I could feel the warmth of his skin radiating lightly against mine and I shivered slightly. I hadn't expected him to actually let me choose whether I kissed him or not, but he didn't kiss me. Instead, he waited patiently for about five seconds before pulling back and smirking. "He looked pissed. It was kinda funny."

I nodded mutely.

Brady chuckled quietly. "You're blushing."

"No, I'm not. That's makeup."

"You poured red paint all over your face and called it makeup?"

"Shut up, Brady," I sighed.

He laughed and turned my body so my back was to him, then pulled me against him so that I was leaning lightly against his chest. I stiffened, and he noticed. "Calm down, Anika," he muttered. "You're acting like I'm just gonna have sex with you right here. If you didn't notice, I'm exercising self-control and haven't even actually kissed you. So I'd appreciate it if you calmed down and stopped treating me like I'm a murderer."

I nodded and forced myself to relax against him. Suddenly, I realized what he was doing. By being on the couch, there was no one else against me, and I was actually a lot calmer than I would have been outside or just standing in the living room. Because of the way my body was angled now, there was no room for anyone else on the couch but him and me. Surely that wasn't his intention, though. This had to be part of his stupid plan. There was no reason for him to be nice to me. Why would Brady Morrison do something kind for me?

We sat there for a while and eventually, I ended up really relaxing, just watching the other people at the party.

Brady leaned down to talk into my ear again. "I bet the first person to throw up will be him," he said, pointing subtly to a boy with red hair who was grimacing a little and touching his stomach.

"I think it's gonna be her," I contradicted, pointing to a girl.

"Are you serious? She looks fine."

I didn't say anything.

He paused. "I bet five bucks it'll be the guy."

"Deal."

Roughly ten minutes later, there was a chorus of protests as the girl I had pointed out doubled over and threw up. Brady groaned and shifted his body, searching for his wallet. He handed me a five dollar bill. "How could you tell?"

"I guess I'm just more used to remembering drunks than you are," I muttered.

"I doubt that."

"You'd be wrong again if you did."

Brady pushed me lightly. "We're gonna go dance."

"No... we're not."

"Look. It's my party. I'm gonna dance, and if it's not with you, it's gonna be with some random girl. That's gonna put you in danger, not me. So it's your choice."

I sighed.

He looked at me expectantly.

"Fine."

# Chapter 4

Brady led me by the hand to the backyard again, and several people brushed up against me as we passed them. As soon as we were in the backyard, I noticed that most of the people from the party had now migrated there as well. They were all talking loudly, and at least two people were touching me at all times because of the crowd. My breathing quickened and my hand tightened on Brady's unintentionally.

He looked at me in confusion and I refused to meet his gaze, ashamed that I was being affected this heavily by something as common and basic as a crowd of people. Finally, he looked away from me again and released my hand, turning to face me. "Do you know how to dance?"

"No." My pulse sped up as I felt someone bump into me again and I clenched my teeth. They were all loud and my head was starting to hurt from all of the noise.

Brady looked at me for a long time. "Go sit down in that chair. I'm gonna go get your water bottle."

I looked at the chair he was pointing at. It was relatively far away from people, and I nodded before walking over to it and sitting down. I brought my knees to my chest and tried to be as small as possible to avoid anyone else bumping into me. Taking a deep breath, I began to calm down a little. As long as I wasn't exposed to more of the pushing and shoving, I should be okay, I remember thinking. A boy approached me and grinned, clearly drunk.

"You wanna swim?" he slurred.

I shook my head immediately. "No."

He grabbed my hand anyway and pulled me out of the chair. "Come on, it'll be fun." The boy yanked me toward him and grinned down at me. I tried to pull away from him, but he was strong. Suddenly, he threw me over his shoulder and I screamed. He laughed as I started thrashing and screeching and carried me toward the pool. I was going to drown. He was going to throw me, and I was going to drown. I kneed him as hard as I could but he didn't respond to it, so I kicked him, hard. This time he groaned sharply in pain and flinched, his body curling defensively.

This almost sent me into the water.

Suddenly, the boy and I were both yanked roughly away from the pool. The boy's hand was gone from my waist, and though I started to fall immediately, another set of hands grabbed me and pulled me off him. Brady pushed me lightly behind him—toward the pool, to my dismay—and turned to face me, guiding me back toward the chair he had originally told me to go settle in.

I sat down, pulled my legs back up to my chest, and immediately began freaking out. Sure, some people called them panic attacks, but I'd never liked the term. My breathing was fast and shallow, and I couldn't uncurl my body from how I'd positioned myself defensively.

Brady's eyes were wide. "Holy Hell, are you dying or something?"

I shook my head the best I could and tried desperately to control my breathing.

He clearly had no idea what to do.

I inhaled and held my breath, then released it, and continued doing that for about five minutes before I was taking reasonable breaths. Brady looked relieved when I was breathing normally again and he offered me my water bottle. I took it gratefully and slowly drank from it, leaning my head forward so it rested on my knees. "Sorry."

Brady's voice was surprised and kind of angry. "Sorry?"

"Yeah."

"Why are you sorry?"

"Because I panicked like that."

28

"It wasn't your fault, it was his, and I'm damn near ready to go back over there and beat him for it." Brady's voice shook a little in anger.

"He didn't know I can't swim."

"It doesn't matter."

I rested my chin on my knee so I could look at Brady, and I was surprised by the intense anger on his face. "Calm down, okay?" He probably was angry at me for panicking and almost causing a scene in the middle of his party. "I said I was sorry for reacting like that." Brady cussed under his breath and stood up.

"I changed my mind, I'm gonna teach him a lesson."

I stood up to protest but dizziness hit me like a train and I almost fell over. Brady's hand flew to my shoulder to steady me. "Can... you go get Mitchell?" I managed. My mind was suddenly very fuzzy, and I was getting dizzier. "I think I need to go." My tongue felt wrong.

Brady said something, but I couldn't hear it.

The strength in my legs was waning and the world was spinning a little. My vision blurred and faded at the edges.

He was almost completely holding me up now, and his eyes were wide as he spoke. I could tell he was yelling but I still couldn't understand what he was saying. It sounded like he was underwater. A moment later, I registered hitting the ground and he was crouched over me, still yelling.

I blacked out.

***

When I opened my eyes again, I was looking up at a ceiling. There was a siren somewhere in the background, and I sat up quickly, only to instantly regret it. The headrush was severe.

"Be more careful, would you?"

I looked at Brady. "What the hell happened?"

"You got drugged, I think."

Chills spread through my body, leaving me with a cold, empty feeling.

"Please don't throw up like you did last time I told you."

"What?"

"You passed out, like, three hours ago in my backyard, then woke up and threw up about an hour ago and passed out again. Try not to throw up this time, if you can." He walked over to the bed I was lying on and looked down at me. "Do you feel okay?"

"I was drugged," I repeated blankly.

"Yeah."

"Um... What are the sirens?" I had only just become aware of them, and they weren't helping my headache.

"Foster found the guy that drugged you."

"... And?"

"And that's an ambulance. No one's gonna say it was Foster that beat him though; I doubt anyone wants to die that badly." He caught sight of my face and quickly amended his statement. "He didn't kill the guy. Just beat him pretty badly."

I closed my eyes again. Tonight really was a disaster. I'd ruined his party and Foster had definitely helped. I'd only drunk from *my* water bottle, though, hadn't I? "Sorry."

"I swear to God, if you're apologizing for being drugged, I'm going to let Foster in here."

My eyes were open instantly and staring at the furious face of Brady. Jeez, I knew I screwed up the party, but why was he so angry? He could just throw another one, right? His blazing eyes almost made me flinch.

He took a deep breath then smirked a little, though the smile held no warmth to his face. "He does want to see you, though."

"What?"

"Foster. He's outside the door, likely listening."

I groaned. "Just tell him I died."

Brady laughed and stood up from his crouching position. "Well, I think you're okay now. As long as you don't pass out again. If you really want me to keep Foster out, I will."

30

"I think he'll break your door, so let him in, I guess."

Foster opened the door instantly and stood there, sizing up Brady for a moment. Brady finally lifted an eyebrow and gestured toward me carelessly, stepping to the side slightly to show Foster he could pass him. Foster walked closer and let his eyes skim over me. "Are you okay?"

"Sure. I think I'm good, other than some bumps and cuts."

"Bumps and cuts?" he repeated.

I sat up too quickly again and my body fell limp against the bed in response to the dizziness. Foster wrapped his arm around my lower back; I hadn't even seen him move close enough to do that. He helped me sit up and glared at the bed.

"I didn't beat him enough," he growled.

"If he's in an ambulance, I think you beat him too much."

Foster smirked. "We've been talking for about a minute and you haven't cussed at me."

I snorted. "Go to Hell, Foster."

He laughed and smiled at me, almost encouragingly. "There's the Anika I know."

Wait. What the hell? I was making him laugh? This was the creep that was *stalking me*. So why was he acting so… *normal* right now? And friendly? "You're acting weird. Did he beat you up as well? Or did you just attack him without his knowing?"

Foster snorted. "I'm too relieved to act weird."

I fought the urge to roll my eyes.

Brady cleared his throat and I looked up at him. He seemed angrier now, even though he'd clearly been on edge for several minutes now. "Hey, if you could get your hands off my girlfriend, that would be great."

Whoa. What? We were only pretending, and it wasn't like Foster was hurting me. In fact, he was helping me with my ability to stay sitting up. So what was up with Brady? "He's not doing anything wrong," I muttered, glaring at Brady a little. I didn't like Foster, that much was true, but that still didn't make it okay for Brady to just snap at him like that without reason.

Brady turned and left, closing the door without a word.

Foster watched and chuckled.

I glared at Foster. "Shut it, creep."

He grinned at me innocently.

I sighed quietly to myself and looked at the door Brady had just slammed. "Boys are completely insane and unreasonable. In fact, the only one I can really stand being around anymore is Mitchell." Realization hit me at the mention of my friend. "Oh, God," I groaned. "He must be freaking out. Where's Mitchell?"

Foster looked at me blankly.

"Mitchell. The guy that I play fight with, who you almost tried to assault in the hallway."

His gaze darkened. "I really don't like that guy. He's a creep. When he touches you, I want to skin him alive. It should be him you're so freaked out by, not me. I'm much less likely to harm you."

"Stop being such a weirdo. You were being tolerable until now."

Foster sighed. "*Mitchell*," he sneered the word as if it was a cuss, "is downstairs panicking. The annoying blonde is throwing up in a bush, or she was last time I saw her. Apparently, she throws up when she's scared."

I grimaced. She really did; I'd learned that on a rollercoaster.

He moved and sat on the edge of the bed, looking at me.

I scooted away from him a little and the arm he'd been supporting me with left to take my hand. It made me flinch; his hand was warm and soft, and its size almost covered my hand, but it was *Foster*. Him touching me was just... wrong. So why wasn't I stopping him? I guess drugs were really as behavior-changing as people said they were. Was that why he didn't seem too creepy to me right now? Because I was so out of it?

"You know, you actually did scare me," said Foster.

"You scare me." There was a little truth to that.

He laughed quietly. "I never was very good at dealing with girls."

"Maybe that's because you're insanely possessive over someone you've only known for two days. It's totally unrealistic to lay claim to me. If you seriously want a girlfriend, turn that shit down, a lot.

32

There are lots of girls at the school that were dead set on getting your phone number. But didn't you say you were taken?"

"I've been taken for years. By you."

"I'm not sure what you have, but I'm certain it's hard to pronounce. I hope there's medicine for it. You should look into getting some."

Foster rolled his eyes.

My head pounded furiously suddenly and I slapped a hand to my forehead, rubbing it, barely managing to suppress a groan.

"Are you okay?" asked Foster.

"I'd ask for water if I hadn't been drugged last time I did."

His eyes wandered over my face for a moment and he leaned in, swiftly kissing my forehead then standing up and walking to the door. "I'll get you some water, and I promise you it won't contain anything other than ice." I stared at him as he pulled open the door and stood there for a moment, contemplating his words. Finally, without looking at me, he started speaking. "You and your friend Mitchell… Neither of you are very good actors." He closed the door behind him and disappeared into the hall.

Uneasiness flowed through my body. What did that mean? Did he know I wasn't really dating Brady? And what the hell had he meant about Mitchell? I massaged my temples for a moment. Who *were* these boys? A bipolar creepy stalker, a player that gets pissed off over nothing…

My world had been turned completely upside down in only two days.

# Chapter 5

Neither Brady nor Foster texted me on Sunday. It was quiet mostly, except for everything going crazy in my head. I'd been thinking nonstop about yesterday. After Mitchell had come to get me and drive me home, I'd seen Foster watching us from the doorway with his fists clenched. Brady hadn't come back after slamming the door. I guess he was seriously pissed about me ruining his party. Now I was lying on my stomach across my bed, with my arms dangling off one edge and my legs dangling off the other. There was a "ping" on my phone and I looked at the pop-up. It was from Mitchell. He'd sent me a video.

I clicked on it and watched the screen curiously. Normally when he sent me videos, they were of cats failing or instant karma. My heart sunk through the bottoms of my feet when I saw Foster on the thumbnail of the YouTube video. I clicked play and saw Foster stalking slowly toward a boy.

"You."

"What? Me?"

"I saw you and—" the audio was muted for a moment and I wondered for a minute why Mitchell had edited this part out; maybe he'd said my name? "—wanna try me?" Foster suddenly punched the guy in the throat, sending him flying backward. The boy got up quickly and swung at Foster, missing. By the time I was five minutes into the video, Foster was untouched and the boy's face looked like he was starring in a horror movie. Finally, the boy stayed down and someone screamed. Foster kept punching him, and it took three guys to finally drag him off the boy he'd knocked unconscious. Foster looked up, dead into the camera. His face when he saw the camera

34

was even more hateful than it had been when he was beating the guy. Then again, who wouldn't be pissed that their fight was caught on camera, something that could be shown to literally anyone?

I felt like I was going to be sick. The video suddenly cut when he started to say something else and I scrolled to look at the comments.

**lol this has to be fake, he looked like right at the camera. plus, who fights that good?**

**That freak went to my school last year... I'm so sorry for this boy...**

I tossed my phone onto the carpet and let my head fall forward so that I was upside down again. Foster was definitely terrifying. He'd just kept beating the guy... and the look he gave Mitchell...

Something hit my back and I screamed.

My cat yowled in protest and jumped off of me as I rolled over.

I breathed a sigh of relief and closed my eyes. Why was I so jumpy? Because of Foster? It wasn't like he was here. He couldn't hurt me from wherever he was.

As long as I stayed away from him, I was safe.

\*\*\*

When I walked to lunch on Monday, I was mildly surprised to see Brady with some girl against him. They were making out—hard. I felt a little sick. I hated it when couples made out like this in the middle of the hallway. Then I realized what was wrong with this: he was meant to be pretending to date me. So was he pretend cheating on me too? Was I meant to be angry about that, or was it even something I was *allowed* to be angry about?

*Oh, for the love of...* They were against my locker.

I walked up to them, not sure of whether to just push them or say something. So I cleared my throat and raised an eyebrow at Brady. "You're in the way of my locker, you know," I sighed when he stopped mauling the girl long enough to look at me.

The girl glared at me, gave him a very obvious, very gross, French kiss then flounced off, swaying her hips as she walked.

35

I snorted as I watched her leave and looked at Brady, who was still against my locker.

"Oh, I'm sorry. Did that bother you?" he asked.

"Why would it? I just don't like it when couples kiss in public, especially at school. School isn't the time or place to be mauling someone. And in front of my locker is *especially* not the place to do it. Don't you have sex under the bleachers sometimes? Why couldn't you just go there with her instead of here?"

His eyes narrowed. "Are you calling me a manwhore?"

I burst out laughing, forced into doubling over from the laughter after a few moments. He was looking at me in confusion when I managed to breathe, and I just barely managed to repeat, "*Manwhore.*" I started laughing again as he glared at me. Finally, I steadied myself and grinned at him, still finding the term funny. "No, that's not what I was talking about. I was just offering you some advice: location, location, location. If you're gonna walk around kissing random girls, just don't do it in front of my locker or in front of Foster. Other than that, you can do what you want."

Brady narrowed his eyes at me angrily and suddenly got really close to me, looking down at me with fury in his eyes. "Well, it's not like I can do that with you."

I raised an eyebrow slowly at his defensive statement. "I didn't ask *why* you were doing it, Brady."

He glared at me more.

I sighed. "Look, I know we're only fake dating. It's okay if you want to kiss other girls. It doesn't bother me."

"Maybe it should," he muttered.

"What?"

He stepped away from me and exhaled sharply. "You're infuriatingly weird, you know that?"

"Yes, actually. You've called me a freak before; yelled it, technically, before throwing things at me and running away." The amusement was gone from my tone and I waited, looking at him challengingly as I remembered him in fifth grade.

His breath hitched, and hesitation interrupted the anger in his eyes. "You seriously remember that?"

"Yes. Why wouldn't I? That's how I met Mitchell."

Brady's gaze slipped away from mine and he looked at the locker for a minute.

I shrugged. "It was stupid. And I met Mitchell, which was great." I smiled at him, trying to get him to smile. "So in a way, I'm glad it happened like that."

His eyes snapped to mine.

I was strangely startled and almost jumped at the way he looked at me so suddenly.

"I have to do something," he muttered, turning on his heel and disappearing down the hall.

Sighing, I started to open my locker. I smiled suddenly as I remembered that day at school.

*It was recess, and I'd passed Brady Morrison a note to meet me outside. Now, I was standing in front of him in my black hoodie and jeans. He looked up from where he was looking at the ground and looked at me. "Um... what did... you want, Anika?" He and I had never really talked to each other before, but he was really cute, and he sat with the special needs kids when they were alone. One time, he'd even helped me pick stuff up when I'd dropped it.*

*"Jamie told me you have a crush on me."*

*"What?"*

*"That's okay, though. I have a crush on you too." I smiled at him encouragingly. I'd never had a boyfriend; maybe he could be my boyfriend. Then we'd date through high school and college and grow up and have kids. Love was probably like that, wasn't it? To feel all nervous and shaky when you talked to them?*

*"I do not!" he exclaimed, turning dark red.*

*I stared at him as my hopes fell away. "What?"*

*"I don't have a crush on you, you freak! Why would I have a crush on a girl that sits alone all the time? I want to date someone really pretty and popular. Not someone like you!" He looked around for a moment and picked up a handful of rocks. He tossed them in my direction and turned around, running away in the opposite direction.*

*I felt tears rise in my eyes. Oh. He didn't. But... I did.*

*"Are you okay?"*

*I turned around and looked at the boy standing behind me. I'd seen him play some kind of board game by himself a lot; I was pretty sure his name was Mitchell and he was holding the board he carried around with him all the time. He looked at the ground. "Um... yeah... I'm... okay," I lied, starting to cry as the words left my mouth.*

*Mitchell's eyes widened and he offered me his hand suddenly, almost shoving it at me with the awkward force he'd used. "I'm Mitchell."*

*"I'm A-Anika," I managed between quiet half-sobs.*

*He smiled at me. "I know. Do you want to play chess with me? I can teach you to play if you want me to."*

*Suddenly, I wasn't sad anymore. I smiled at him. Maybe I'd fall in love with him now instead of Brady. Glasses were kind of dorky, but kind of cute, right? He didn't have a lot of friends, so there probably wouldn't be any competition for his attention. He was the polar opposite of Brady. Instead of rumors about him having his first kid, like Brady, the rumors about Mitchell were that he had done something really bad and that's why he came to this school now. But he looked way too sweet for what people said, and he was being nice to me. What could possibly be wrong with playing a board game with someone? "Sure, I'd love to play. I won't be any good at it, though."*

*"We have lots of time. I can teach you."*

*I smiled at him and sat down, watching him set up the board and point to different pieces, naming them and telling me what the different ones could do.*

Mitchell, *I repeated in my mind. That was a good name. He was good, even though the other kids said really bad things about him. Even if I didn't fall in love with him, he would be nice to me, I thought. Not like Brady. He wanted to date pretty girls, not girls like me. That was okay, though. I'd fall in love with someone else now.*

*I didn't need him.*

I laughed quietly to myself as I remembered how unreasonable I was in fifth grade and pulled open my locker, taking out my wallet so I could go buy lunch. Boys never really did grow up, did they? Sure, he hadn't thrown anything at me this time, but Brady had just

38

called me a freak and run away again. An eleventh grader did the same thing a fifth grader did.

"Hey, you wanna walk to lunch?"

I turned around to see Mitchell. "Yeah."

Maybe it was good some things didn't change.

***

Foster was at my table when I walked to it, and he was eyeing Mitchell.

"Would you quit looking at him like that?" I sighed.

"Like what?"

"Like he killed someone. Mitchell's a nice guy. You don't have to keep acting like a paranoid weirdo whenever you see him." I sighed. "I really wonder what you're like when you're alone if you're this creepy around other people. It worries me."

He smirked. "You wonder about me?"

"Of course that's all you got out of that statement."

Foster grinned further. "Was there anything else in the statement?"

Moron. I started nibbling on the pizza I'd bought without much interest and I could feel Foster looking at me. "What do you want now?" I groaned in defeat, giving in to his gaze.

"Nothing. I enjoy watching you."

Kind of sweet?

"Especially when you don't know I'm watching."

Nope. Creepy. Just creepy.

I ignored his statement and continued eating my pizza. When I looked up a little, I realized Foster had his sleeves pulled down over his hands. "What's wrong with your hands?"

"They hurt."

"From what?"

"Beating the shit out of that scumbag that drugged you." Foster's tone darkened as he reminded me of the weekend. "I should have hurt him worse." He looked up at me, his tone lifting suddenly. "They don't hurt too bad, though."

I leaned over and pushed his sleeve up.

His knuckles were really beat up. There were a few scars littered around his hands, but the relatively fresh scabs and bruises made them look... awful. I couldn't help the gasp that escaped my lips, and Foster shrugged, pulling his sleeve back down. "Like I said, it doesn't hurt too bad." He smiled a little at me.

This boy was so weird. He went from creepy to normal, to creepy, to kind, to creepy again. What the hell?

I pulled his hand toward me so I could inspect it further and moved his fingers gently to uncurl them, looking them over. The cuts weren't too deep; in fact, it just looked like he scraped his knuckles on sandpaper or something kind of roughly, and the bruises were beginning to fade a little bit. "I guess you're okay," I decided eventually. "Don't just walk around beating things up though. Violence is only the answer sometimes, and this was not one of those times."

When I looked up, his gaze was intense, and I was immediately uncomfortable with touching him. He drew his hand back slowly, still looking at me, and covered it with his sleeve. "I'll be sure to be more careful next time, then."

Mitchell cleared his throat. "I'm here too."

I looked at him and smiled. "Like I'd forget you." I leaned over and put my head on his shoulder for a moment to reassure my friend then went back to eating my pizza. "Brady's being weird," I blurted randomly to Mitchell, almost forgetting Foster was there.

"How so?"

"I don't know. He brought up some random thing from fifth grade. Er... I guess I did, kinda. But it was because of something he said first."

Mitchell stopped moving. "Some random thing?"

"When I met you. I told him that because I met you I was happy that things happened the way they did, but he was still acting weird about it." I shrugged.

"That's no random thing," he growled.

40

"I said I'm happy it happened that way," I replied, defending myself.

"I'm glad it happened like that too."

"I'm still shitty at chess."

"That's because you still call knights 'the horse ones' and pawns 'the short ones'. If you just try, you'll get it." He shook his head, chuckling. "Six years and you still don't know a bishop from a pawn." I was happy he'd let go of his irritated tone. Mitchell wasn't usually intimidating, but that voice could kill if he wanted it to.

"Do too. One's a castle and the other one's short."

"The things you say almost make me cringe."

I grinned at him and looked at Foster. "Do you play chess at all?"

"Yes."

"Really?"

Foster snorted. "Try not to sound so surprised, would you? I *do* have hobbies."

"Are you any good?"

"Very. I'd like to play against Mitchell sometime."

Mitchell's eyes flashed up to Foster, catching my attention. For the first time in six years, I saw hostility in his eyes. "I'd like that as well, Foster. It's a battle of wits, after all."

I looked between the two boys. When Mitchell caught me looking at him, the hostility was replaced by friendliness. "Boys are crazy," I muttered, sighing quietly to myself.

"Maybe that's 'cause you drive them crazy," Foster snorted.

I glared at him.

"Hey, what class do you have after this, Mitchell?" I asked suddenly, hoping we could walk together.

"Actually, we both have Honors Cyber Security Three," Foster piped up.

Mitchell's arms tensed, the hostility returning to his face. "Yes. We do. Though I do have to say, your ability to code is weaker than my own. You should work on it."

"I intend to," replied Foster.

41

All three of us fell into an uncomfortable silence, and I prayed that Sierra would show up soon to relieve me of babysitting duty.

Stupid boys.

# Chapter 6

*Foster*

I looked down at my phone screen and smiled. I'd only recently hacked Anika's phone cameras, and I really didn't regret it. Right now, she was watching a video and her mouth would twitch every so often in amusement. It was rather fascinating to watch.

I loved watching people who didn't know they were being watched. When someone is alone, that's when their actions are purest; free of the pressure of acting how they thought they should. There is nothing in this world more beautiful than purity.

"Foster, would you mind giving me a summary of the passage?"

Sighing softly as I was pulled away from enjoying my video, I started explaining. "Basically, Hermia just found out Lysander's been cursed to love Helena, and Demetrius is cursed to love her too. They're fighting, Helena thinks it's a joke and that they're both in on the joke." I looked up at the teacher and raised an eyebrow. "Is that close?"

"Alright. Just try to look like you're paying more attention."

"Sure." I snorted. I read Shakespeare classics in my free time, so for us to be reviewing *A Midsummer Night's Dream* was relatively pointless and insanely dull. Pressing a few buttons, I switched my camera view to check in on Mitchell.

He had his phone in his pocket or somewhere else dark.

There was something seriously off about this guy. He was... weird, and creepy to say the least. Not creepy enough to scare me, and somehow not creepy enough to scare Anika, but creepy enough to get my attention. I narrowed my eyes at the screen. In two days, I hadn't seen him on his phone once. There was something weird about that.

Finally, the bell rang and I stood up to go to lunch. It was the only period of the day I saw Anika other than Astronomy and I cherished spending time with her, even if she had that moronic jock hanging around her half the time. She deserved a lot better than him; just a week ago I'd caught him in the hall kissing some random girl. I'd thought when Anika saw it, she would freak out and dump him, but I'd left before I had the chance to see how she reacted. As long as she was happy, though, I wasn't going to interfere.

For now.

When I approached, Anika's face was on the lunch table and she looked like she was sleeping until she lifted her head and banged it on the table lightly. Even though I knew it wasn't hurting her, it bothered me that she did that when she was annoyed. I sat down across from her and waited for her to acknowledge my presence.

"What are you doing, Foster?" She sounded tired.

"What does it look like?"

"Like you're sitting."

"Strange; that's what I'm doing." I snorted and let my eyes travel over her. She was wearing a large hoodie, but it wasn't one that I'd seen in her closet. Where had she gotten it? It definitely didn't look new.

"Give me my hoodie, Anika," Brady sighed as he approached behind her.

Jerk. If she'd taken one of my hoodies, I'd have let her keep it as long as she wanted.

But when she pulled off the hoodie, I definitely wasn't complaining. Her tank top was very... generous. I couldn't help but stare at her as she removed the item of clothing, and I was pretty sure I wasn't the only one watching. Brady's mouth damn near fell open. What? Had he not realized how beautiful she is? He was seriously making my blood pressure rise. Girls weren't beauties who only deserved to be appreciated when there was less clothing on their

44

bodies. A feeling of being watched pricked me and I casually slid my gaze from Anika to the cafeteria door.

Mitchell.

He was watching the table and I saw a flash of something in his hand.

Immediately, I reached and pulled out my phone. The camera was still black. He must have blocked me when he found a virus on his phone; that's why I wasn't able to see or hear anything on his end. I stood up angrily and stalked toward Mitchell. He looked mildly surprised by me approaching and I shoved him roughly against the door. "What the hell do you think you're doing?" I asked as calmly as I could manage, only being pushed further into my annoyance when he smiled faintly at me. "I'm pretty sure Anika wouldn't appreciate it if she knew you were taking pictures of her without her knowing."

"For Christ's sake, Foster!" Anika snapped.

I hadn't realized she was watching me. Mitchell's smile suddenly fell away and was replaced with a look of fear as he looked up at me. "He was taking pictures of you."

"Mitchell and I have tons of pictures of each other! And he's on the yearbook committee!"

If he was taking yearbook photos, wouldn't he be using an actual camera rather than a phone? Either way, the hate in Anika's voice was acidic enough to almost make me flinch. Almost. I looked at her, then back into the artificially fearful eyes of Mitchell, and Anika's hands went to my arm, trying to pull it off Mitchell.

Her hands on my arm made my entire body tingle.

I looked down at the small girl trying to pry me off of him and I released him reluctantly. If she hadn't asked me to let go, I wouldn't have. But because it was her...

"You seriously need to stay the hell away from us!" Anika growled as she pulled Mitchell out of my reach. The smile returned to his lips.

Anger rose in my throat. I wanted to yell at her and tell her that there was something seriously wrong with her little buddy; that I knew there was something wrong with her relationship with Brady.

45

I wanted to tell her that she needed to trust me because I knew a lot of things she didn't and that if she didn't let me protect her, bad things could happen to her. Just take the party for example; she hadn't gone with me, and she'd gotten drugged because of it. I suspected there was something else going on with that, though now wasn't the time to bring it up. "Anika," I said slowly through my teeth, barely managing to contain my anger, "you don't understand."

"No, Foster! *You* don't understand!"

I stared at her blankly.

"Mitchell is my friend! You're not! So leave us both alone." Her voice shook angrily and the look in her eyes was painful to see.

Brady walked up behind her, and he was clearly sizing me up. "Is there a problem, babe?"

*Babe.* The way the word rolled off his tongue made me see red. I couldn't hurt him, though. If Anika wanted him, I couldn't hurt him. The second he hurt *her*, on the other hand, he was done. If she found out about him kissing some random girl, it would destroy her. So, yet again, I suppressed the words threatening to tear their way from my throat. I looked at Anika again. "I'll leave for now. But I'm not going to leave you alone forever, Anika."

Her jaw clenched and I turned around, walking away.

I wouldn't lie to her, and I wouldn't disappear from her life again. I couldn't. So even though the last thing in the world I wanted to do right now was walk away from her and leave her in the way of danger, I had to do it.

As I walked down the hall, I contemplated my options. I could beat Mitchell into submission, but he would tell Anika. Or she'd figure it out herself; she was smart despite how socially ignorant she appeared to be sometimes.

I could tell her about Brady, but that would cause her pain.

My hands were tied and it made me furious. There was something off about all of this.

And I was going to figure out what it was.

# Chapter 7

*Anika*

I glared at my food furiously. What was Foster's issue? He'd almost hurt Mitchell *again*. His anger problems were starting to become *my* anger problems.

"Hey, I'm okay," Mitchell said gently from across the table.

I looked up at him; I hadn't realized my eyes were tearing up. Why the hell was I crying? It wasn't like he was actually hurt, and Foster hadn't threatened me. So why was I so upset that Foster had gone and acted like a raging bull again? I closed my eyes and laid my head on the table. Brady's hand touched my back lightly, rubbing in small circles. The only reason I didn't cut his face off for touching me when I was angry was that it felt kind of nice; the warmth of his hand was comforting. I lay like that for a long time, just soaking up the silence and enjoying the relaxation which contrasted so heavily with the chaos that my life was becoming. "I'm seriously done with this entire school," I muttered, more to myself than anyone else. "The only sane guy here anymore is Mitchell."

Brady's hand stopped momentarily but rubbed my back again lightly a second later.

"Sorry," I muttered, realizing I'd probably offended Brady. "I'm just annoyed. The whole 'pretending to date you' thing is stressful, and now I have to watch Mitchell all the time to make sure that he's not being murdered by my new stalker. It's not his fault this is happening, but he's still being terrorized because of it."

Mitchell kicked me lightly under the table and I looked up at him.

He smiled at me encouragingly. "I said I'm okay."

"I'm not," I growled. "He's on my last nerve."

"Then just cut him off," said Brady. "Don't talk to him if you aren't seriously in need of something you can't get from anyone else." His voice was weirdly hostile. "I'm sick of him too. He seriously needs to back off. If you need anyone to come make sure he's not stalking your house, I'd be happy to oblige. I have nothing better to do."

"That'd just alert my parents. They're watching the cameras and stuff on the house since they're in Washington right now. I think I'd rather have Mitchell at my house."

"Why?"

"He's been my best friend for six years. I can't tell you how many times he's spent the night with me. My parents love him." Mitchell smiled at me and I gave him the most convincing smile I could manage in return. Brady had a faraway look in his eye and I was pretty sure he wasn't looking at me anymore, rather through me at something else.

When I looked, there was nothing behind me. "What in the world are you looking at?"

"Nothing," he muttered.

I smiled at him the best I could.

My phone buzzed and I groaned inwardly. Was Foster seriously trying to talk to me? I ignored it and sat up, taking a deep breath. He needed to leave me alone. He needed to think I was seriously with Brady, and he needed to realize that I would never be interested in him. I couldn't believe what I was about to ask, especially since I had rejected the idea of him being at my house literally less than two minutes ago. But the buzz of my phone just reminded me that I needed to stick to Brady for now. "Brady, can we go on a date tonight?"

He looked at me, startled. "What?"

"A date. That thing couples do."

"Why? You seriously want to?"

Not really. "Yes." I just wanted to get my point across.

Brady grinned at me, a reaction I hadn't really expected. "Sure, that sounds great. What do you want to do?"

"I don't care. Anything that'll keep me busy for a few hours."

Mitchell cleared his throat. "Take into account who you're talking to, then reevaluate the statement you just made."

I realized what Mitchell was hinting at and heat filled my face as I glared at my best friend. "I'm going to kill you someday." Still, though... "How about we just watch a movie or something then just go somewhere else to hang out?" My phone buzzed again and I sighed sharply, finally looking at it. Surprisingly, the texts were from Sierra.

**hey, foster just passed me looking like he was gonna kill someone.**

**anikaaaa replyyyyyy**

I sighed. I hated it when she spammed me.

Instead of replying, I smiled at Brady. "You can come over whenever. Text me first, though."

Brady leaned in and kissed my cheek lightly as I stood up to leave. "You bet."

This was going to be interesting.

***

"Leave, Foster."

He raised an eyebrow from where he was sitting in my car. "No."

"What do I have to do, start spraying all of my stuff in pesticides and hope those are strong enough?"

"Pesticides are for pests."

"You *are* a pest."

He snorted.

"I'm going to invest in Anti-Foster someday. And it's just going to be really, highly concentrated mace. Like, bear mace."

Foster waited patiently, ignoring my comment. "You still haven't given me a good reason to move, Anika."

"Look, I have a date with Brady later, and I really do not want to bring you with me." I sighed. "Brady and I have been together for three months, and you're seriously beginning to make me feel like you're trying to split us up, something I don't want to happen. If you would kindly leave me alone, that would be wonderful." Why was I even bothering to ask? It's not like he was going to actually listen to me. He never did. There was no telling what was going on in that weirdo's head.

"Kiss me."

My mouth fell open. "What?" That was basically the last thing I thought he would ever say to me right then, especially after I'd just threatened him with bear mace.

"Kiss me, and I'll leave you alone if you want me to."

"I'm not kissing you, you creep."

He smirked. "Then I'm not leaving you alone. I offered you a way to get me to leave you alone, and whether you take it or not is your choice. I have nothing to do with your choice, technically."

"You're insane."

He smiled. "No matter what you do, I'm not going to stop, Anika."

"You sound like a serial killer."

"Maybe I am. You're not trying to find out if I am or not." His voice suddenly flattened and his ever-black eyes seemed to glitter faintly with something resembling... hurt.

I felt a slight pang of guilt. Was he offended? "Maybe if you stopped trying to force yourself on me against my will, I'd be willing to try to know you," I conceded eventually.

Foster stared at me. "What?"

"If you stopped freaking me out all the time, I would probably consider befriending you."

"Really?"

"I don't see why not. When you're not acting like a crazy person, I actually like you. You seem smart and relatively kind, despite how creepy it is that you're obsessed with me and trying to make me love you." I shrugged as if it was the most normal thing in the world,

50

trying to use reverse psychology on him; most of the time, guys wanted what they couldn't have, so when they had it, they stopped. Two of us could play that game, if that's what he wanted to waste our time on. "If you try to be normal, I'll try to like you."

He grinned. "Then I guess I'd better get out of your car."

"Good idea."

Foster looked at me one more time, flashed another grin, and got out of my car so I could leave.

Great. Now I was going crazy too. I'd asked Brady on a date and offered to be friends with Foster. Even though I was just doing it to get rid of him, it still felt weird.

What was wrong with the world?

\*\*\*

Brady texted me at five.

**I'll be over in an hour, I have the perfect date idea.**

I smiled despite myself. He was actually going to try this. It was just for fun, but it was nice to know he actually wanted to make it enjoyable for me. Pulling on a shirt over my tank top, I sighed quietly. I'd liked his hoodie. It was huge on me and comfortable enough that I'd "unintentionally" stolen it after he had me hold it for him.

Brady knocked on my door exactly an hour after his text and I was surprised to see him with a stack of movies in his hands when I opened it. He looked from me to the movies. "Er... I wasn't sure what kind of movies you like. So I brought... all of them."

I laughed. "Come on, get in here."

He walked in and looked around a little. "Nice house."

"Thanks. My living room is over here. We can watch the movies in there if you want." He nodded, so I led him into the living room, gesturing for him to sit down and taking the movies from him. I looked through them for a moment and stopped, smirking. "You own the movie *Mamma Mia*?" I asked him curiously, surprised that he owned a romantic musical.

Brady scowled. "I thought chicks liked that stuff."

I laughed. "That wasn't the question."

He sighed. "Yes, I own it. Go ahead, make fun of me."

This confused me. "Why would I make fun of you? It's a movie." His expression changed and I looked down, continuing to search through the discs. "Hmm... you choose. None of them are bad. I'm cool with any of them."

He picked out the one I'd silently hoped he would pick: *The Conjuring*.

I loved horror. I placed the movie in the PlayStation and grabbed the controller, going back to the couch he was on. We sat relatively close, leaving a few inches between us, and I was surprisingly comfortable with it. Maybe it was because I'd already been this close to him before. Either way, the "date" was off to a good start.

The first jump scare, though I'd been expecting it, still got me. I didn't realize I'd flinched toward Brady until I felt his arm come down around my shoulders, rubbing my arm lightly. It was weird for him to act like this; Foster wasn't anywhere near here. Well, hopefully. He held me close to him long enough that when my neck began to cramp, I gave in and just laid my head against him. His head rested on mine as we watched the movie, and it felt... almost natural.

We stayed like that until the end of the movie, and I realized it was getting quite late. I yawned a little and snuggled against Brady for warmth. It was nice to be this close to someone, but as the night dragged on, I was getting tired.

"Are you tired?" Brady murmured.

"No," I lied.

He chuckled. "You're basically asleep."

"No, I'm not."

I'd done this countless times with Mitchell; fallen asleep with him, that is. Because I'd done it before, it wasn't too awkward to be with Brady like this. His finger swirled small patterns on the fabric of my shirt, and it felt strangely soothing.

"Do you want me to leave?" he asked suddenly, his fingers stopping in their place on my arm.

My options were simple. Ask him to stay, or tell him to leave. So why was I struggling with the question so much? It was so simple… but it also wasn't. "You don't have to if you don't want to," I said finally, after a long pause of consideration.

He mumbled something I didn't understand and I felt him turn his face so his lips pressed against the top of my head.

Immediately a few red flags went up. *Whoa. What? No. What? Foster isn't here.* I didn't move, but I definitely felt like reacting. Then again, how was I even meant to react to that? Brady seemed to take this as a sign that it was okay and his fingers began to skim over my arm again in longer, lighter patterns. Maybe I should've asked him to go. This was weird. Why was he acting like this? I mean, I knew he was a player, but that wasn't a good reason to screw with me like this. It was simply cruel to play with a girl's emotions just because he could.

"I'm sorry I kissed that girl," he murmured against my hair. He sounded like he was being serious, another thing that surprised me. Since when was Brady considerate?

*You don't need to be; this is fake, remember? The only reason I even asked you over was because I knew Foster was watching somehow… I mean, it was fun, but…*

"I was just… frustrated."

*So you needed to maul a girl in front of me?*

Brady muttered something else that I missed. Damn his low voice; I missed what he said half the time, I was pretty sure of it. After a few moments, his hand moved from my arm to around my waist. He was being really weird. He was probably just tired or something and not sure of what he was doing. A few minutes later, his breathing evened out, and I was pretty sure he was sleeping.

I looked at the screen which was now back at the title screen of the movie. Maybe I really was going crazy, but the reflection on my TV of Brady and me on my couch was… nice. I shifted a little bit to be more comfortable and closed my eyes. If he was asleep, there was really no escape for me without waking him up, so there was really no point in trying to get out of my fate of sleeping here.

As I lay with Brady, something hit me suddenly. If I had gotten Foster to believe I felt something for Brady, could I have possibly made Brady think I felt something for him? The next question that came to mind following that was even more troubling than the first one:

*Did* I feel something for Brady?

# Chapter 8

*Foster*

I pushed the weight up away from my chest and exhaled sharply. "Fifty-three," I huffed, bringing it back down and pushing it up yet again, "fifty-four," I panted hard and did the last bench press, putting the weight back and sitting up. My arms burned in a satisfying way and I paused thoughtfully. Working out had always helped me clear my head. I'd been considering something for several hours, and now I was certain of what I was going to do. Picking up my phone, I dialed Anika's phone and called her. It was pretty early on Saturday, and I'd been able to work out the fact that she didn't like mornings, but I figured she'd pick up if I called enough times, though it was probably going to bother her. The phone was answered on the first ring, and I immediately felt like something was off.

"Hello?"

The voice wasn't Anika's, but it was annoyingly familiar. I'd been right to think something was happening. "Who's this?"

"Brady. Who's this?"

"Foster."

He was silent, yet I could practically hear the hostility in the silence. Brady was definitely not happy that I'd called her, but I honestly didn't care. I had absolutely no interest in him, other than the irritation I felt about him being at her house this early. "What exactly are you doing calling *my* girlfriend at eight in the morning on the weekend?"

"I'd rather talk to her than you, so if you could return her phone, that'd be great. I trust that she wouldn't be very happy if she knew that you were touching her things."

"No. She wouldn't want to talk to you, trust me. We were sleeping." Anger rose in my throat. He had no right to dictate who spoke to her and who didn't. There was a quiet female voice on the other end and Brady spoke again. "It's just Foster. I figured you wouldn't care." Again a muffled voice. "Because you were sleeping." Her voice rose and they began arguing. Suddenly, Anika's voice replaced Brady's.

"What, Foster?"

She was angry, but I was pretty sure it wasn't because of me. "I want to see you today."

"Okay."

I was startled. She wasn't going to argue against it? She must be super pissed at Brady to not even hesitate about meeting up with me. Either way, I was excited to see her. "Okay. Meet me at school, and we'll go from there. Sound fair?"

"Sure, whatever."

Brady was yelling in the background, and Anika's line went dead within seconds. Anger flooded through me again. He didn't have the right to yell at her. *I* didn't even yell at her, and I had to watch her be happy with someone else. That's what love was, after all: wanting the other person to be happy, even if it didn't include you. He didn't love her. I could tell he might think he did, but he didn't.

I took a deep breath as the fresh anger brought more energy to my arms.

I lay back down and started doing bench presses again. If I was going to be calm enough to talk to her, I needed to work out and waste the extra energy I had before I saw her.

*＊＊＊*

Anika was standing outside the school, just like she said she would be. She was in one of her normal outfits—just a hoodie and jeans—and I almost smiled at the sight of her. Her small frame against the

56

brick of the school was such a welcome sight. Her head was lowered, but I didn't take much notice of it until I got closer to her. Was she... crying?

"Anika?"

She looked up at me instantly. Her eyes were red.

That scum made her cry.

I was going to kill him.

After I'd calmed her down, though. Right now, I was too concerned to leave her alone. I got close to her and bent my knees slightly to lower myself so that I could look her directly in the eye. "What's wrong, Anika?" My voice was low and gentle.

She shrugged.

"Don't give me that."

"I'm not actually dating Brady," she muttered.

"What?"

"I was never dating Brady. Honestly, I didn't even like him before you came to the school. He offered to help me keep you away from me, and I said yes." Her eyes brimmed with pain, but she smiled at me with quivering lips that proved to me the falseness of her smile. "It's okay, though. Because that's over. I'm sorry I tried to get away from you so badly, and I'm sorry I lied to you."

"I don't care about that. Don't apologize."

She looked at me, half with disbelief. "You seriously don't care that I lied to you?"

"No."

"Why?"

"Because you can never do anything wrong in my eyes." I smiled a little. It was the truth. There was nothing she could do to permanently leave me angry with her; not after what she'd done for me. This was the girl who had turned my entire life around. The disbelief in her eyes grew a little and she looked away from me. I hooked my finger under her chin, lifting it so she faced me again.

"I'm sorry," she murmured again.

"I told you not to apologize. You will never have to apologize to me, Anika. I can promise you that."

She looked up at me and I was thankful to see that the tears were gone from her eyes. God help Brady if he ever went near her again. Anika smiled a little at me, then looked away again. "I call you creepy a lot, but I think you're just not sure how to express yourself, so it comes off as creepy. I mean, you should definitely tone down the obsession part, but..." Her blue eyes looked into mine and I felt a slow energy grow within my body.

"But?" I prompted.

"But... you've never actually done anything bad to me."

I wanted to tell her that I was physically incapable of doing anything to harm her. I wanted to tell her that I'd waited to see her again and thought about her often and that it had been a miracle for her to still be in this town at all, but I refrained so she could finish speaking.

"I'm sorry I judged you. You seem nice. Just a little confused." She tilted her head, then she did something that completely shocked me. Anika stepped closer to me and wrapped her arms around my lower back, pulling me closer to her and into a hug. I straightened up immediately and my heart raced as she let her head rest against my chest. She'd never actually gone out of her way to touch me before, let alone in a way that was affectionate. "Can you forgive me?"

There was nothing to forgive. "Yes."

"Friends?" she checked.

"Friends."

\*\*\*

We stayed at the school for a couple more hours after that. It was relaxing to be with her and not have her telling me to leave her alone. She didn't even cuss at me. Brady must have really screwed up to have her change like this, but I was kind of thankful for it. I knew there was something off about their relationship, but I was almost sure that they were really together. I figured they were just not very compatible and going to break up quickly. Did this make me right?

Anika looked at the school from where we were now standing by my car.

58

I watched her. She was just so fascinating to watch. Maybe once she got over Brady, I could make her realize that she belonged with me. If I could get her to see that, I wouldn't need to hack her phone and computer cameras anymore, because I would just keep her with me all the time. The idea of having that kind of relationship with her made me smile out of nowhere, but she didn't notice. She was too busy looking at the school.

"I don't like it here," she murmured after a while.

"What do you mean?"

"I don't like it. The people here hardly know I exist, and the ones that do..." She closed her eyes. "I want high school to be over. The only reason I stayed here when my parents moved to Washington to take care of my grandparents was that Mitchell and Sierra are here and I couldn't even fathom the idea of leaving them here alone. I mean, I don't want to sound like they need me or anything, but I still don't think it would be fair of me to leave them behind like that. I just... want it to be over, I guess."

I nodded. It was understandable to make statements like that when she was upset.

"When I was in fifth grade, I thought I loved Brady," she stated suddenly, opening her eyes but not looking at me. "Then he called me a freak and told me he wanted to date pretty girls. We never really talked, but he was kind to me before that, and I wasn't really used to people being kind to me. That's when I met Mitchell. He offered to play chess with me, and I said yes. I even lost the game to him on purpose so he would keep teaching me because I didn't want him to go away. After that, I met Sierra. She was just so happy all the time, I thought if I was around her enough, I could be happy like that too. The three of us were friends all throughout middle school, but now things are changing again. Mitchell hasn't been around as much as he used to be. He just holes himself up in his room with his electronics when he leaves school. He hasn't challenged me to chess in weeks. That can't be healthy, right? Sierra basically avoids me. Brady became part of my life out of nowhere, and then he was gone again. Everything is going backward now. First Sierra left, then Mitchell, then Brady. Everything is going in reverse, and I don't want it to."

Listening to her and the sadness hidden behind her calm tone, my heart broke a little. If that pattern was right, I should have been the first one to leave. Though, technically, I guess I had. I turned and looked down at her more directly.

She looked up at me in a slightly confused manner, and I dipped my head to get closer to her. Her breath hitched, but she didn't stop me.

So I kissed her.

# Chapter 9

*Brady*

I walked into my room and slammed the door behind me. I was physically shaking from anger. Anika. It was always Anika that got me this riled up. She'd broken it off with me out of nowhere and gone to meet Foster. And what do I get for going to try to find her and ask her to talk about it? I see her kissing him.

*Him.*

The boy she asked me to keep away from her, the boy who stalked her intensely, the boy who I had promised to keep her safe from, the boy with anger problems and a terrifying personality.

The girl who asked me for help, the girl who told someone we were dating, the girl who had been completely controlling my every thought for over a month, and the girl who refused to kiss me because she had never been kissed before.

I took the nearest thing to me and threw it as hard as I could against the wall, satisfied by the thud the wall provided in return.

A lot of people said their life flashed before their eyes when they were about to die. For me, every time I had ever been near Anika life flashed before my eyes because of how angry I was.

Her in fourth grade wearing pink all the time. Her in fifth grade wearing cute little dresses and wearing her hair in a braid and confessing she had a crush on me. Her in sixth grade getting pushed around by some guy who I'd beaten the hell out of later that week for touching her so he'd never go near her again. Her in seventh grade with two friends who weren't me, even though I wanted to be around her. Her in eighth grade wearing a brand new hoodie and changing up her hairstyle to wearing it in a bun. Her in ninth grade with headphones and a "screw off" attitude that drove me crazy, even though I didn't talk to her. Her in tenth grade, only sitting with the two people she'd met in sixth grade and not talking to anyone else. Her in eleventh grade, curled up on a couch with me after our first real date. Her this morning, yelling at me for answering her phone and crying as she finally snapped from all of the stress she'd been under. Her a few minutes ago, pressed up against Foster and kissing him as if he was the one she wanted to be with.

Everything I'd ever seen her do was flashing before my eyes, and I couldn't stand it. All the girls I'd used to distract myself from her, the girl I'd kissed to get her attention, all of it was for nothing because she was never going to want me and I couldn't do anything about it. I'd always known she would never stay with someone like me when she was... *her*. That didn't make it any less excruciating to deal with now, though. That made it so much worse. Knowing that I had known she would move on and that I had still gone for her when I knew it would end like this.

She thought this guy was in love with her. She thought that obsessive stalking and possessiveness over someone he barely knew meant that he was in love. She was choosing him over me, and I had known that she would pick someone over me eventually.

Anika.

Anika.

*Anika.*

The name mocked me mercilessly and I threw something else. I felt like screaming.

The only girl I'd ever truly cared about was leaving because I was too much of a coward to stop her from doing it.

# Chapter 10

*Anika*

I stared down at my lap as I sat on my bed. My head was spinning. Sierra was pacing in front of me, trying to sort through what I'd told her. Even though she'd been avoiding me recently, she had still come to my house when I called her. Sometimes I really loved the people I knew.

"So you kissed Foster."

"He kissed me."

"How long did it last?"

"I don't know, ten, twelve seconds?"

"Then you kissed him back, trust me." She sighed. "Okay... and what happened between you and Brady?"

I stiffened. "Why do you think something happened between Brady and me?"

"Because you kissed Foster. That means you completely abandoned the idea of dating Brady to keep him away from you. Either way, you're basically pinned to Foster now. You'd better pray that Brady doesn't find out, Anika. He'll throw a fit."

"Like he cares," I muttered.

Sierra raised an eyebrow at me and, when my expression didn't change, she threw her hands up and looked at the ceiling. "She's completely clueless. I'm not sure what to do with her!" she announced, still looking at my ceiling. "Please, for the love of you, tell me what I'm meant to do with this stupid female!"

I glared at her. I hated it when she pretended to talk to a third party when I was right here.

Finally, Sierra returned her gaze to me and grabbed my hands. "Sweetie, I'm going to try to say this as kindly as I can manage so that you don't freak out, alright?"

"Okay."

"You're a moron."

"That wasn't very kind."

"It was the best I could do."

I sighed and let myself fall backward, staring up at my ceiling. Everything from yesterday was fresh in my mind. I'd woken up to the sound of Brady's voice, which was nice at first, but after a few seconds, I had realized he was using my phone.

*"Who's that?" I asked, sleepily.*

*"It's just Foster. I figured you wouldn't care."*

*"Why didn't you give me the phone, then?"*

*"Because you were sleeping."*

*Annoyance coursed through my body. I hated it when people touched my things without permission, and I especially didn't want people snooping around on my phone. "What the hell, Brady? You can't just answer my phone like that and not tell me! Give me my phone!"*

*Brady held the phone away from me and I leaned over and snatched it anyway. "What, Foster?" I snapped tiredly.*

*"I want to see you today," said Foster.*

*"Okay." Good. I didn't want to be with Brady right now; he was just invading my personal space without asking. We weren't really dating. He had no right to just go through my things without permission. At least Foster was open about his creepiness. What right did Brady have to use my stuff while I was sleeping?*

*"Okay. Meet me at school, and we'll go from there. Sound fair?"*

*"Sure, whatever."*

*"Are you serious, Anika?" Brady yelled.*

*I hung up the phone. "What?" I snapped.*

"I answer your phone, so you agree to go on a date with some creep? That's how it's gonna work? You'd better let me come with you! He'll try to pull something if I don't!"

"So what if he does? You're not my boyfriend!"

Brady stared at me furiously. He couldn't deny it; he really wasn't my boyfriend. His jaw clenched and unclenched over and over as he fought for something to say to change my mind. "That's bullshit and you know it, Anika," he growled at me eventually.

"Do I?"

"You should!" he yelled.

"But I don't, okay?" I yelled back. Tears stung my eyes. I'd spent all night wrestling with my feelings, trying to figure out exactly what I felt for him. Why I was so comfortable with him. Why I let him spend the night. Why I liked him when he'd never done anything to make me happy. "I don't know anything!" My voice trembled and the anger was wiped clean off his face as he realized I was about to start crying. He reached toward me and I jerked away from him. "Don't!"

He stared at me, the anger threatening to return but not fully showing in his eyes. "What the hell changed between last night and now?" he asked as calmly as he could, his voice dangerously low and painfully confused. "Tell me what changed. Did you not want me to spend the night with you? I would have left if you had just asked me to. Were you not okay with me wanting to have an actual date with you? I wouldn't have pushed you to do it if you didn't want to." His voice shook a little and I bit down on my tongue to keep from crying.

I didn't know what I felt. Between Brady, Foster, the date, the waking up, the phone, and the certainty that all my friends were leaving me because of them, I just couldn't handle all of the stress that was forming. I felt like I was going to be sick if I kept yelling at Brady. A few tears escaped down my cheek and Brady's face twisted.

"Don't. Don't cry." I was shaking with all my pent-up emotion. Brady stepped toward me before I could react and pulled me against his chest. "Please don't cry," he whispered. "Please. I don't want you to cry, Anika. I never wanted that."

*I shook involuntarily. My body trembled against his and he rocked gently side to side, just enough that I could feel it. Under normal circumstances, I would have been happy for that kind of affection when I was this upset. But the fact that it was Brady that made me feel like this in the first place was ruining that. I didn't want him to be touching me right now, though I didn't really feel like pulling away either.*

*"Shh..." he whispered. "I'm sorry I yelled at you."*

*This made me shake harder. I wanted to be angry with him, and be a complete bitch, and not feel bad about it. All of the frustration from the past two months was coming out now and I felt horrible for unleashing it on Brady, but I couldn't help it. He was being so kind to me for no reason. He had no reason. He wasn't my boyfriend, he didn't love me, and he had no interest in me or my life or anything about it before that day in the hallway, so why was he being so damn kind to me?! "I want you to leave, Brady," I whispered against his chest.*

*He stiffened. "You want me to leave?"*

*No. "Yes."*

*Brady's arms slipped away from me after a moment of hesitation. "Okay," he said simply.*

*And he'd left.*

Remembering this brought fresh tears to my eyes and I gritted my teeth. It had been fourteen hours since my fight with Brady and I was no closer to figuring out what I felt for him than I was when we argued. Talking with Sierra hadn't really gotten me far at this point, and Mitchell hadn't answered the phone when I called him. God only knew what he was up to. I didn't dare call Brady to explain myself, and it wasn't like I could talk to Foster. As soon as he'd finished kissing me, I'd told him I had to leave, and he had accepted that.

He looked happy, at least. At least there was one person I wasn't disappointing right now. When he'd told me that I couldn't do anything wrong, I'd been so thankful to him for lying to me. So when he tried to kiss me, I let him. I didn't really want to kiss him, but I just didn't want to see disappointment on yet another person's face. I was so tired of disappointing everyone with anything I tried to do anymore, so I would be damned if I'd let another person hate me. The only thing in my life that was certain anymore was...

I messed up.

***

Brady didn't call me on Sunday, and neither did Mitchell or Foster. Sierra was still at my house though. She had spent the night so she could hear more about Brady and me, and I had ended up crying again when I told her about the fight. She wasn't great with advice, but she was perfect for providing a realistic view of things.

*"You've known Brady for how long? I can get why you'd be upset about him answering your phone and all, but realistically you shouldn't be this... sad."*

She was right. I shouldn't be this worked up over him.

But I was.

I stared up at my ceiling, thinking about what I could do. There was no confronting Brady, at least not now. The chances of me talking to Foster right now were the same as the chances of me finding a dolphin in my bathtub. Mitchell wasn't talking to me right now. Basically, my only options now were to have Sierra relay a message or leave things the way they were.

My phone rang on my dresser and I groaned. "Sierra, can you get that?"

Sierra nodded and picked it up. "Hello? Oh hey, Mrs. L. Yeah, she's here... No, I don't think she wants to talk to anyone right now..." Her face paled. "What?" She turned to look at me. "Um... you think she would want to do that? I mean, if she were... no, yeah, I understand that, but... seriously? Seven months? Okay, okay, I'll have her call you when she's up for it. I'm sure she'll give this serious consideration."

She hung up and looked at me. "Um... your mom wanted to ask you something."

I looked at her, tired. "What did she want?"

"Well..." Sierra hesitated uncertainly, capturing her lip between her teeth as she did and she never finished the sentence.

"Sierra," I prompted.

The next sentence she spoke after that changed everything.

I had another choice.

.

# Chapter 11

I looked at my ceiling blankly for a while. It'd been a week since my mom had called me, and I still hadn't told anyone but Sierra about it. I wasn't going to say anything until I knew what my answer was. This was my choice, not theirs. No one else could choose this but me. My eyes slid closed. I didn't technically need to give my mom an answer for weeks, but I did need to make a choice.

Stay or go.

***

Thunderous knocking startled me awake and I shot to my feet immediately, shoving myself toward the door. When I pulled it open, I was looking up into the furious eyes of Brady. *Sierra, I don't know where you are, but I swear to God I am going to kill you if I survive this.* "What do you want, Brady?" I asked uncertainly.

"You think you can just move without telling me?"

*Screw you, Sierra.* "It's not your choice."

"It affects *me*," he growled, "so I think I should get a say in it."

I looked up at him, my fury growing almost to match his. "You *don't* get a say in it!"

He took a deep breath. "Can I come in?"

"No."

Brady pushed through my bedroom door anyway and ran his fingers through his hair. Why did he even bother to ask when he was going to do whatever he wanted either way? "How can you just… try to leave me like that?" he demanded. "You're selfish, you know that? You're making a choice that's going to affect more than just you and you're not asking for input from anyone." His free hand shook at his side slightly and his jaw clenched immediately once he finished talking.

I looked up at him blankly. "Try to leave you?" I repeated.

He closed his eyes briefly, his hand still lodged in his hair, then pushed against me suddenly, pinning me against the door. My heart pounded wildly as I searched his face for answers as to what he was doing. His hands were on my waist now and he was holding me in place. "You might think none of it was real," he murmured, his eyes open now and searching mine, "and you might not feel anything for me. But I'm so tired of just watching you do things without being a part of it, Anika. I'm so tired of not doing something about what I feel. You can't just leave. I won't let you." His lips crushed against mine suddenly and fire shot through my veins. Brady pushed me against the door with his hips as he kissed me roughly.

I couldn't think, and I'd closed my eyes at some point. I couldn't see him, but I could feel him. His heat was everywhere, and my body was reacting without me telling it to. My arms went around his neck after a moment and I kissed him back easily.

When he finally pulled away, it left us both panting hard. His breath gently washed over my face as we stood there, unmoving and silent. Brady's hand cupped my cheek lightly and his thumb brushed over my face, making me shiver a little bit. His other hand remained on my waist, and he pressed his lips to mine, more gently this time. The fire flooded through my veins as Brady kissed me again. "Please don't leave," he managed at one point before kissing me a little harder. His lips forced mine apart and he deepened the kiss.

I shivered hard, but it made me happy. My fingers tightened a little in his hair and he made a soft noise against my lips, catching me off guard and sending heat to my cheeks. Finally, he pulled away again. I kept my eyes closed, but I could feel him watching me, searching my face for how I would react to him. But how *was* I meant to react to this? It made me feel…

"Anika," he breathed quietly, "please tell me what you're thinking."

70

"I don't know what I'm thinking." My mind was completely blank.

His forehead touched mine gently.

"I can't really think like this," I murmured.

Brady's thumb traced over my cheekbone in smooth strokes. "Can you at least tell me if it was okay that I did that? That... I kissed you?" The worry in his voice wasn't well hidden. He was actually afraid that I was going to reject him. I'd never heard him so vulnerable, but while I enjoyed the kiss, it just felt...

In response, not letting myself overthink, I gently pressed my lips to his again.

He made another quiet noise, but this one sounded more relieved. His body relaxed against mine as he kissed me back and the hand that had been against my cheek slid down to my waist again. My body reacted so differently to Brady than it did to Foster. He made me feel warm, but Foster made me feel dizzy. Kissing Brady was definitely nice, and I could get addicted to something like that easily if I had enough time, but when Foster had kissed me, it was entirely different. The ground hadn't shifted, there weren't fireworks, but it felt easier. More natural. More genuine.

When he pulled away this time, I had sorted out what I felt. "I think I have a crush on you again, Brady." Even if Foster was easier for me, I still wanted fireworks. Foster was a gentle, steady feeling, while Brady was a flash of fire. Would that be good for the long term, though?

He laughed, and I could feel the smile on his lips when he kissed me again. "I have a crush on you too, Anika," he replied in a slightly teasing tone. "I just wish I would've told you six years ago when I realized it the first time around instead of waiting."

I shivered lightly.

"Please don't leave me," he murmured.

"I won't," I found myself promising.

But I wasn't sure I meant it.

\*\*\*

Two hours later, Brady still hadn't left my room. We were lying on my bed now, with him drawing small circles on my back with his finger lightly while we talked. After all, we did have a lot to talk about. I explained why I kissed Foster, he told me why he kissed that girl in front of my locker intentionally like that. "Were you actually considering moving?" he murmured quietly.

"Yes."

He fell quiet for a few moments. "Why?"

"My grandpa died, but my parents don't want to move back. And living on my own for a year might not be so bad, I guess, but I was torn between leaving things the way they are and actually letting myself start a new life because I was confused." I traced my finger over his stomach gently to distract myself. "I'm not confused anymore." My finger trailed over the fabric of his shirt, lightly going over the lines of his stomach. Apparently, I'd distracted him too because his hand stopped and his skin trembled a little under the shirt. Did I seriously have that effect on him?

He shivered lightly and I continued swirling my finger across his tummy.

Eventually, I settled my hand on his stomach and stopped moving, relaxing against him again.

Brady exhaled slowly. "Don't do that again."

"Why? Did I hurt you or something?"

"No. I'm just… male, if you're catching what I mean."

I waited for him to explain further.

"You're so innocent," he groaned.

I snorted. "I'm a walking innuendo, actually."

"I'm male," he repeated. "And you're female. And I'm a teenager. And you're a teenager. And we're lying together, and you started touching me in a way that—"

"Enough!" I squeaked. "I understand!" My face flooded with heat as I realized what he was saying.

He snorted.

Brady started tracing circles on my back again. "So does this mean we're actually dating?"

"Do you want to?"

"Look at me."

I tilted my head back to look at him and he swiftly maneuvered his body so that he was on top of me and kissed me slowly. My lips worked against his and eventually, his lips forced mine open like they had earlier. Within moments, our tongues were battling for dominance and I suddenly understood what the appeal of French kissing was. He kissed me a little harder and I blushed. Once I realized exactly what we were doing, I pushed on his chest gently and ignored the confused expression he had. "I... um... super virgin."

He started laughing and buried his face against my neck. "If I was trying to have sex with you, you would've known that by now, Anika." His breath against my neck sent chills through my entire body and I shivered. Brady noticed. "Wow. You're easy to affect."

I glared at him a little, but when he brushed his lips lightly against my neck, my entire body went almost numb. "B-Brady...!" I stuttered in warning.

He laughed again and rolled off of me, pulling me against him by the waist. "I know, I know. Super virgin. I won't forget." Brady rubbed my side gently as we lay there. "You know, I really liked spending the night with you. I don't think I've actually ever slept with a girl without... you know, *sleeping* with her. It was actually really nice." His tone was thoughtful and reflective, and I was pretty sure he didn't intend to make me as annoyed as he did when he said it.

I poked him in the ribs and he flinched.

"Hey!"

I snorted and snuggled against him.

"Jealous, are we?"

"Arrogant, are we?"

"You know it." I could hear the grin in his voice and shook my head, rolling my eyes.

Boys were morons.

Something unsettling caught my attention, though. Technically, he hadn't said yes to wanting to date me. He'd simply kissed me.

That was no different from what he'd done with any other girl, and suddenly, I didn't feel as secure with our placement.

# Chapter 12

A hand nudged my shoulder lightly.

I grumbled in protest, snuggling closer to the warm body next to me in the bed, unwilling to move away from my comfortable position beside Brady.

"Anika," a voice whispered.

I ignored it. If someone seriously wanted to wake me up right now, they were going to lose the damn hand they were touching me with, especially if they stayed within reach.

Brady grumbled sleepily.

His voice was coming from a different direction from the first voice. Chills shot up my spine and I sat bolt upright immediately and stared at Foster in disbelief. "How the actual hell do you know where I live, Foster?" I yelled. "And why the hell are you in my room? How'd you even get in? I lock the doors here!"

Brady was awake instantly and sat up as well.

Foster raised an eyebrow at Brady then turned his gaze back to me. "Your spare key is under the plant holder, third from the left. It's not a great hiding place." His eyes traveled over me for a moment, and he didn't even glance at Brady. "I've only been standing here for a few minutes, anyway."

I groaned angrily. There was no dealing with this guy. I lay back down and yanked the covers over my head. Maybe if I just stayed like this long enough, he'd disappear.

"Come on, get out of bed."

I'm pretty sure Brady was in shock because he hadn't started yelling yet.

"What the *hell* Foster?"

Oh. There it was.

Foster snorted. Slowly, I pulled the blanket off of my head as I realized what he was here for. "Oh. Yeah. That." He smirked at me lopsidedly and I groaned in disapproval of his being there. "I just want to sleep in!" I groaned, rolling over and pulling a pillow over my head.

"No, Anika," he said patiently, "you promised.

"I hate your memory," I growled into the mattress.

"Promised what?" Brady asked finally. The tone of his voice was enough to almost make me flinch.

"Anika said that if I left her alone until today, she'd let me spend the day with her. I imagine you don't know it's her birthday today, given the way you're acting." Foster's tone was not nearly as patient or kind toward Brady, though it wasn't really angry either. Not giving him a chance to reply, Foster's hand went to my lower back and rubbed in small circles. "Come on, I have a really fun day planned."

There was the sound of a slap and Foster's hand was gone.

Oh, God.

"Don't touch her," Brady growled.

"I don't listen to you."

"You're going to when I wipe that smirk off your face."

"Try me."

I kicked Foster, then rolled back over so I was almost in Brady's lap; I hadn't realized that he was facing Foster now. His face was stony, and his jaw was set when I looked up at him. I forced myself to sit up despite my desperation to just sleep in for once. "Look, I get to choose how I spend my birthday, alright? So *you*," I said, pointing to Foster, "go downstairs. I'll deal with you in a moment."

He smiled at me easily and slipped through the doorway, shutting it behind him.

I forced a heavy sigh out of my chest. "This is my life now," I muttered as if to force myself into believing this was my reality as I moved myself out of bed. As soon as I was on my feet, though, Brady pulled me gently down and onto his lap. My face burned with heat as I looked at him, searching for a reason as to what he was doing.

"You didn't tell me it was your birthday today," he murmured.

"Yeah... that's because I don't like celebrating it that much. All I did was not die."

"You're eighteen now, right?"

"Yeah."

He nodded a little bit and I felt him smile as he lightly pressed his lips to my neck.

I shivered and stood up a little too quickly, looking at him. "I'd tell you to go downstairs if I trusted you not to start something with Foster, but I don't, so you're going to stay right there until I'm done getting ready. Then I'm going to spend a few hours with him." Brady's face twisted into a scowl and I held up a finger to keep him from talking. "Ah, no. You have no place telling me what to do, alright? I'll text you when Foster's finished whatever he has planned, then we can spend the rest of the day together, and I'll be with you tonight if you want."

His face lit up immediately. "Okay." His smile changed slightly, though, and I realized the wording of what I'd said. I dismissed the way his smile had changed.

I stretched and walked over to my dresser, pulling out a tank top, an overshirt, and some jeans. "I'm gonna go shower," I announced before kissing Brady lightly on the cheek. Since my parents were in Washington, the master bedroom was mine, and that meant I had a bathroom in my bedroom. As I walked into the bathroom, I clicked the lock. It wasn't that I didn't trust Brady not to peek... but I didn't.

"Oh come on, you're locking it?" he whined from the other side of the door as if to confirm my suspicions.

I snorted and ignored his protest, slipping off my clothes and getting into the shower. A few moments later I could hear talking, and it was getting louder. So, after washing the last of the shampoo out of my hair, I walked to the door.

"So what if I *was* in the shower with her?"

"I'd have to beat you senseless."

"I'd like to see you try."

"If I come out of this bathroom and you two are fighting or injured in any way, I'm making both of you leave," I called through the door. Immediately the two boys fell silent and I wrapped a towel around myself to peek out of the bathroom.

Brady was glaring at Foster, who was seated at my computer desk with his hands behind his head. Foster's eyes flickered over to the door when I opened it a little and he chuckled before turning his eyes back to Brady. By the time I'd looked back at Brady, he was already looking at me and we made eye contact.

"Just checking," I muttered before closing the door.

Once I'd put on the tank top and jeans, I walked out of the bathroom.

Brady's eyes widened a little bit. "Um. Are you seriously going out like that?"

I looked down at myself. Since I never dried my hair, my tank top was basically drenched, but I couldn't see his problem with it. "No, I'm gonna put on an overshirt when my hair dries, why?"

His eyes darted away. "Too hot," he muttered.

Heat flooded my cheeks again. "Excuse me?"

"You look too hot for me to trust Foster around you," he explained, without looking at me. I noticed his cheeks were a little tinted. Holy Hell. Was Brady *blushing*?

Foster had his eyes set on me, I could feel it. I could always feel it when he looked at me.

I looked at him and was pleasantly surprised to see that he wasn't looking at me with anything other than mild interest. His eyes slipped away from me again and I snorted. It was a tank top, not me walking out of the bathroom naked. Not like Brady seemed to know the difference between the two. "You're making me self-conscious," I informed Brady eventually.

"What?"

I sighed quietly. "Never mind."

Slowly, Brady's eyes came to settle back on me.

Heat touched my cheeks again, but I ignored it. I laughed and sat on the bed next to him. Foster was looking at me again, but I just laid

78

my head on Brady's shoulder. It clearly annoyed Foster a little bit, but the guilt I felt was quickly pushed aside when Brady spoke.

"Babe," he groaned, "you're getting my shirt wet."

I removed my head, pouting.

Foster smirked; I could hear it in his voice. "You could always come sit with me, Anika."

Brady made a point of wrapping his arm around my waist and pulling me more tightly against him. His arm was tense and defensive, and his eyes were guarded.

I sighed. "You're both morons."

Foster's smirk didn't falter as I looked at him. "How so?"

"The things you two think baffle me."

Brady turned his head and kissed my forehead. I saw a flash of anger in Foster's eyes and his hands twitched in his lap. "Go dry your hair and get this over with so you can come spend your birthday with me, okay?" he murmured to me quietly.

I nodded and stood up, returning to my bathroom but not daring to close the door again.

When I'd finished, I could feel Foster watching me. Jesus. Did he have to do that all the time? I snuck a glance at them. Brady was lying on my bed on his back, staring at his phone, but Foster's eyes were set on me. Interest lined his face as he watched me and I returned my gaze to the mirror, picking up my makeup bag and pulling out some eyeliner and mascara to touch up my eyes.

Once I'd finally finished my makeup and hair, I returned to the room. "Done," I announced.

Brady sat up and stared at me, his eyes traveling very slowly over my entire body, up and down. He didn't seem to notice the blush in my cheeks, or rather, he didn't care because he continued to just stare at me.

Foster stood up and grabbed my hand gently in his, flashing a look at Brady. "Come on, you ready?"

"Yeah, let's go," I said, slipping my hand out of his as subtly as possible. "Go downstairs. I want to pick a shirt to wear over this tank top." Foster nodded to me and walked out of the room like he had done earlier. Brady had gotten to his feet at some point, but I hadn't noticed until I looked over at him. I walked over to him and tilted my head. "Are you okay?"

"I don't trust him," he growled.

"He's going to get bored eventually, Brady," I assured him. "Besides, it's just me hanging out with a friend." His eyes flashed at the word "friend" but I ignored it. "It doesn't matter if you can't trust him; you trust *me*, don't you?"

Brady seemed to battle himself internally for an answer. "I guess."

"Good." I kissed him on the cheek and smiled.

"Wear my hoodie, would you? So he doesn't forget that you're with me."

I took his hoodie obediently and slipped my phone into the pocket, smiling at him as reassuringly as I could. "Okay, I'll take your hoodie."

"The only thing that could make you look sexier in my hoodie is if you weren't wearing pants right now."

I blushed and smacked him in the chest. "That wasn't the question."

"You were distracting me."

I laughed. "I wasn't doing anything."

"You don't have to." Brady leaned in and gave me a lingering kiss, his hand on my lower back pressing me against him lightly. "You should probably leave now or I'll be tempted to try to make you stay here with me instead." I nodded and turned, smiling at him one more time.

"I'll be back soon."

Brady didn't reply. Instead, he sat down on my bed again and turned back to his phone.

I jogged down the stairs and looked up at Foster, sighing internally. "Let's see what you have planned."

# Chapter 13

*Foster*

I was almost shaking with excitement. It didn't matter that I'd seen Anika asleep with Brady, it didn't matter that she was so reluctant to come, and it didn't even matter that she was wearing his hoodie, because she was here now, and we were alone. She hadn't really said anything since we'd gotten in my car, but it was a comfortable silence. It always felt comfortable when I was with her.

Anika had one leg pulled up against her chest and her arms were wrapped around it as she looked out of the window. Even glimpsing her like that was enough to make me smile.

I returned my eyes to the road.

"Why are you smiling?"

"You're with me. Do I really need another reason?"

Anika chuckled.

It was such a beautiful sound when she laughed. Like warmth and happiness mixed with a childish innocence. I wished she would do it more often. Maybe I just didn't amuse her that much. The thought of not being able to make her smile made me feel a little unhappy, but luckily she broke into my thoughts by speaking.

"Where are we going, anyway?"

"First, we're going to see a horror movie. Then I'm taking you to lunch, and after that, back to my house."

She sighed lightly. "For how long?"

"You promised you'd spend the entire day with me," I reminded her, "which means I'm allowed to take as long as I like to spoil you today." The thought of spoiling Anika made my lips curve up again. If she'd just give me a chance, I'd give her anything she wanted. I wanted to shower her with gifts and make her happy however I could, all in the hope that she would someday look at me as more than... What did she even see me as at the moment? A friend? Whatever we were, I was ready when she was to make it something more. "You like horror movies, don't you?"

"Yeah. How'd you know that, though?"

If I told her about the camera on her television I'd managed to hack, it would ruin the moment. "Wild guess. You strike me as someone who would enjoy them." It always burned my tongue when I lied to her, but I couldn't quite be completely honest, either. She found it 'creepy' that I wanted to keep her safe, but that's all it was.

"Good guess."

"Thank you."

We sat in silence for a little longer. "Why are you being so... normal?"

"Excuse me?"

"You're being... normal," she repeated. "Like, you're not threatening to kill anyone, or looking at anyone like you want them to die, or saying anything creepy. Are you sick or something?"

"I'm just at ease when I have you to myself, that's all."

Anika didn't reply, and I peeked out of the corner of my eye to try to guess what she was thinking. Her brows were pushed together a little bit, but they smoothed out quickly enough and her lips twitched upwards.

Today was my chance.

***

After gently insisting that I pay for both her movie ticket and the snacks, ignoring her vast complaints about me doing so, we'd found our way to a pair of seats in the middle of the theater. Now we were roughly halfway through the movie, and none of my attention was on it; instead, I was watching Anika. During the jump scares, her eyes would widen slightly and her lips would part just enough to gasp. When the son had been killed, her eyes had teared up a little. She was so much more fascinating than a movie could have been. I'd never really enjoyed horror, personally, since I knew the basic formula of making a decent horror, but watching her watch it made it worthwhile. The different emotions flickering across her face in response to whatever was happening was just too intriguing to ignore or not take notice of. I was holding the popcorn bucket, but I hadn't really eaten much; popcorn didn't interest me. It was more of a reason for her to be closer to me than anything else.

The music grew slower and began to build up, something I knew meant a scare was coming. I placed my hand strategically on the armrest we shared and, when the scare happened, her hand flew to mine and grasped it tightly as she jumped.

She didn't seem to notice, or rather she didn't mind, but either way, her hand didn't leave mine for the rest of the movie. My skin was warm where she was touching it, sending warm shivers of pleasure through my body. I hadn't thought it possible to be this happy from someone touching me just a tiny bit, but it was. Because it was her.

At the end of the movie, her hand slipped from mine and I pouted internally. Anika grinned up at me as we made our way out of the theater. "That was such a good movie! I didn't see half of the jump scares coming, and when they did, the effects were so detailed I would have thought it was real!" The enthusiasm in her voice brought a smile to my face. Her eyes glittered with excitement as she spoke, and she was gesturing with her hands. "I mean, seriously, when she got that acid dumped on her, I legitimately thought they'd dumped acid on the actor from the way the effects worked and how she reacted! The fact that there was no romantic subplot made it a lot better for me, too. I hate it when two people survive just because they served as a subplot."

I nodded. There was really no need to reply. She was too excited to notice my silence; not that I minded.

"That might be my new favorite movie of all time," she decided. Finally, once we had reached my car and I'd opened her door for her, she looked up at me and into my eyes. We'd hardly ever made eye contact, and when we did, I felt electricity coursing through me. "Thanks for the movie, Foster. I'm sorry I thought this wasn't going to be fun."

My chest fluttered a little bit and I smiled down at her. "Anytime, Anika."

She smiled at me again and sat down in the car. I closed the door behind her and worked my way around to the driver's side. This was perfect. This was how it was meant to be. Me, her, and happiness. I never wanted the day to end.

Anika talked nonstop about the movie on the way to the restaurant, and I listened closely. When she spoke, I couldn't do anything other than soak up every word of it. She finally looked out of the window and blinked a few times in surprise. "Italian?"

"Yes."

"You're probably the most accurate guesser I've ever met."

Well... sure. It could be considered that. "I do my best." I smiled at her and we got out of the car. When we got inside, I let Anika pick the table, and she slid into the booth quickly.

Her eyes were so alight it was mesmerizing. How could one person be this perfect? I hardly noticed the waitress when she came over, giving her my order and keeping my eyes on Anika. "She's very pretty," Anika noted suddenly, sipping her soda.

I raised an eyebrow, completely unsure of what the context was, despite the fact that I was paying attention, or so I thought. "Who?"

"The waitress."

"I hadn't noticed," I dismissed easily.

Anika snorted. "She definitely noticed you."

"Meaning what, exactly?"

She laughed. "Meaning she was trying to flirt with you. She looked pretty upset that you weren't taking notice of it, too. Does that happen to you a lot when you go out?"

"I would imagine so, I guess. It doesn't matter to me."

"Maybe if you weren't so attractive you'd appreciate it a little more."

A smile tugged at the corner of my mouth. "You find me attractive?"

"Yes," she said slowly, picking her words carefully. "You're definitely attractive. But me saying you're attractive doesn't mean I want to have sex with you or anything; it just means that I can appreciate the fact that you're kinda hot. I'm not saying that to suggest I don't like Brady, either."

"That makes sense." I smiled at her. The fact that she mentioned Brady bothered me a little, but it wasn't her fault. It was Brady's. He'd been so paranoid about today—rightfully so, I imagine—that he'd probably drilled it into her head to not give me any more attention than she needed to. Anika began sipping on her soda again, and I put the straw to my lips without much interest. The only thing that could even come close to having my attention was her.

The waitress came with our food after a while, and Anika's eyes lit up a little when hers was set down.

I chuckled quietly. Despite the stereotype that girls hated food and avoided it, I knew very well that there were girls that loved food and eating in general. Personally, I'd never really liked girls who refused to eat in front of me. Girls who were willing to eat and just be natural with me were so much more appealing. Anika started in on her pasta, and we ate in silence for a while. Once more, it was a comfortable silence. No words really needed to be spoken between two people who were comfortable with each other, and that was a fact of life I truly enjoyed.

After a while, Anika looked up at me with a questioning look in her eyes.

"What is it?"

"Why are you so interested in me? I'm really not that special."

Hearing her say that made me irritable. If she truly thought that, it meant someone had influenced her to think that way, and it made my stomach churn to know that she didn't see herself the way I did. Then again, the days we had known each other had obviously left little to no impression on her; that much had been made clear on the first day. "Well," I said slowly, thinking through what I wanted to say, "you're… incredible. I watched you and Brady the first day I got there, and the way you just completely blew me off fascinated

85

me. Then in class, when every girl had her eyes locked onto me, you had acted as if I was just another person. I don't get treated like that often, and it was nice to experience. You say things sometimes that keep me thinking for a long time after you've said them, and you're just overall interesting." A smile slipped onto my face as I mentioned not being treated like that often; it was true. With my father's status, it was hard to be treated like a normal person if they recognized my last name before I spoke to them. "I just can't *not* be this interested."

Light pink tinged her cheeks, sending satisfaction through my entire body. She smiled a little and looked down at her food again.

If it wasn't for Anika, I probably wouldn't have ever grown a spine. She was one of the first people in my life to treat me like I was someone worth protecting instead of just a trophy my father had to prove his legacy would continue. It wasn't that I was obsessed with her; it was what she had done for me that had caught my attention. Perhaps initially when I came to visit, I had been in love with the idea of her rather than actually in love with her, but she'd changed that in the past months.

She'd probably be changing a lot more than that if she let me stay in her life.

# Chapter 14

*Anika*

My eyes were closed and I was listening to Foster talk. He was just talking about music, but it was kind of nice to listen to him, even if I wasn't listening to the actual words. His voice was surprisingly nice; I hadn't realized that before. It was smooth and warm like chocolate, and its deep tone was relaxing. When he wasn't being a total weirdo, he was actually fun to be around. I'd almost fallen asleep during the ride because of how soothing his voice was.

The car stopped and I could feel Foster looking at me.

Instead of making him decide whether to touch me or not to see if I was awake, I lifted my head and looked around.

He smiled at me. "We're here."

I stared. This... was his *house*? The 'house' in front of me was roughly twice the size of mine, and I had a nice house. "How many siblings do you have that you need this many rooms?"

"Hm? Oh, I only have the one brother, but he's twenty and living on his own now."

"Right." I stared at the house.

He smiled at me and got out of the car. Foster made his way to my side and opened the door for me, gesturing for me to step out. When I did, he smiled at me again then made a noise that sounded kind of nervous. "Ah... you aren't... intimidated or anything, are you?" he asked slowly. "You look kind of overwhelmed. The house is just a show-off piece that my father wanted if that helps anything. I'm not materialistic."

"What? No, I was just surprised, that's all."

He sighed and touched my waist lightly, nudging me toward the house. "Come on, I'll show you around."

"What do your parents do?" I blurted randomly. Immediately, I wanted to retract the question.

"My father's a major stockholder in a technology business; he builds computers and phones and designs apps. My mother walked out a long time ago, probably five or six years ago." Five or six? He would have been eleven or twelve when she'd left, then. "I do remember that she was a biologist, though." Jeez, his entire family was full of geniuses. "Now my older brother works in security; he designs security systems and helps track down hackers. Personally, I'm not all that interested in electronics, though I do seem to have a knack for playing around on them, as I've discovered recently."

The tone in his last sentence made me a little suspicious, but I didn't ask anything else. That explained the class he had with Mitchell, then.

Foster opened the door and let us in. "My father's out for the day."

"Do you have maids or something? There's no way you maintain all of this on your own." Jesus. Why did I keep asking questions?

He laughed, not visibly offended by my question. "You have no idea how happy I am that you're comfortable with this. No, I don't have maids. And as for your comment earlier, we only have five bedrooms in the house. Most of it is wasted space, honestly. I keep up on maintaining it for the most part. It would be nice to have someone else in the house, though." I felt his eyes wander to me but I was too busy looking around the living room. Though it was bigger, it wasn't any more elaborate than mine was. Foster touched my lower back to get my attention and I jumped a little. Disappointment tinged his eyes. "You don't like it here?"

"What? That's not it. I'm just surprised is all."

His eyes shifted around the room. "Like I said, I'm the only one in the house most of the time. I don't like extravagant luxuries or any of that; they don't make people happier. Really, when I move out of here, I plan to move into a house more closely resembling yours, granted that the person I live with during that time agrees."

I nodded. Something was bothering me about this, though; had he invited me to his house just to show me he had money? He owned an average car and never wore flashy clothing, so there was really no way for me to have guessed it on my own. Why had he asked me to come here?

Foster's hand slipped down to hold mine.

I raised an eyebrow at him. What was he doing?

His eyes settled on the ground, and he shifted a little on his feet. Was he nervous? "I was homeschooled for most of my life, and because of that, along with the straight-out neglect from my parents, I'm socially... strange. I know you find me creepy, but in all honesty, I don't know any other way to interact with someone or show my affection." He took a deep breath before looking at me again, and his eyes were hesitant. "I'm not really the best at anything involving other people, and I'm not great with celebrating things, but I tried to make something. It's not something I think you'll really love, and I struggled a little making what I did make, so..." His voice trailed off.

What was he talking about?

Foster led me to his kitchen and I was surprised to see a small cake on the table. "Like I said... it's not... great or anything, but..."

I hugged him.

He stiffened in surprise at my sudden action, but his arms wrapped around me a moment later.

"That's really sweet of you, Foster. I love it. Thank you." I'd never really celebrated my birthday like this. No one had made me a cake before, not a handmade one anyway, so for him to have made one for me when he seemed so unsure of his cooking abilities meant a lot to me. Because of his height compared to mine, I could hear his heartbeat, and it was rather fast. He seriously had been nervous that I wouldn't like it. I stood on my tiptoes and kissed his cheek gently, trying to be friendly and show my appreciation of the cake and his efforts toward making it. "That was really thoughtful of you, and no one has ever baked me anything. Thank you."

Foster's face was tinged slightly pink but he was grinning at me widely, his eyes alight with happiness. "You really like it?"

"Yeah." I smiled.

We ended up taking the cake into the living room, and it was surprisingly good. For someone who claimed he didn't know how to cook, he sure as hell could. I was able to eat one and a half pieces of cake before I was full, and Foster had seemed thrilled when I'd asked for a second piece. We were seated on his couch now, and he was watching me. He was always watching me.

"I appreciate you letting me treat you today," he said eventually.

Seriously? He'd spent the entire day doing things I wanted to do, and he was thanking *me*? I leaned my head on his shoulder in response and I heard his breath get a little shaky.

"I know you're dating Brady," he murmured slowly, "but I want to let you know that kissing you was the best decision I've ever made."

Heat swirled in my cheeks a little bit.

"I'd... like to do it again, if I could."

My heart sped up. This was why he brought me here, I was certain of it now. He wanted me completely alone in a place where there were no other people, and he was going to try to get me to change my mind and be with him. And yet, I didn't quite feel like it would be a bad thing.

"Not now, of course." His tone was reflective, and it soothed my nerves. "I'd only kiss you again if you asked me to or if you and Brady were no longer together. But that doesn't lessen the desire to kiss you in any way, especially when you're with me like this."

I didn't know how to respond, so I didn't say anything.

"If you want to leave after hearing me say that, I'll understand, Anika. I wouldn't take it personally."

Slowly, I nodded, realizing it would probably be better if I left.

Foster stood up and smiled at me, but he couldn't hide the disappointment on his face, even if it was only in his eyes. "Alright. I'll drive you home, then."

The drive back to my house was quiet. This silence was different from the silence earlier. There was more tension in the air this time. Finally, we pulled up to my house, and I could tell Foster wanted to say something. "I... um, got you something. I know you really don't like receiving things, but I wanted to get you something anyway."

"You already did so much for me today," I murmured.

"I don't feel like it was enough."

I didn't say anything. There was no point in arguing with him; I was starting to understand that Foster was the kind of guy who wouldn't stop doing what he wanted, no matter what anyone said.

Foster pulled out a small box from his pocket and offered it to me. "I was going to get you a hoodie, but I thought that would be a little too obvious."

I took the box and opened it. Inside was a simple but very pretty necklace. It had a normal silver-colored chain, but on it was a dog tag with the word "penguin" written on it in cursive. I'd forgotten about my conversation with him last week; he'd kept asking me questions, and in my desperation to get him to stop, I'd just listed off random facts, one of them being that my favorite animal was a penguin. There was a little penguin engraved into the dog tag as well next to the word. "It's beautiful," I murmured quietly, tracing over the penguin with my finger. "You seriously do listen to everything I say, don't you?"

"Yes."

I leaned across the car and hugged him, kissing him on the cheek again. "You're an amazing friend, Foster. Thank you for everything."

He smiled at me. "Anytime."

When I walked inside, Brady's arms went around me immediately. "He didn't try anything, right?"

I sighed. "He was just friendly."

Brady let out a sigh of relief. "What's in the box?"

"A necklace. He got it for me."

"Can I see?"

Brady pulled out the necklace and his face twisted when he saw it.

"What?"

"It says 'Foster' on it, Anika. It has his name on it. Are you seriously going to wear this?"

"What?" I repeated, taking the necklace from him. Sure enough, on the back of the dog tag, the word "Foster" was engraved in beautiful writing. "I didn't notice that when I took it. On the front it's just a penguin and the word 'penguin'."

Brady's look didn't change.

"Yes, I'm going to wear it," I said finally, realizing what he was waiting for.

"Why? You're mine. Not his."

"Because it was a gift, and I accepted it because of the penguin thing. Plus, I lost my actual penguin pendant a couple months ago, and that was really devastating to me, so I need something else to wear."

Brady went quiet for a moment. "I didn't know you like penguins."

He didn't? Surely I'd mentioned it at one point or another... right? If I'd mentioned it to Foster, I'd definitely mentioned it to Brady. A question that had been bugging me since lunch crept into my mind. "Brady, why do you like me so much?"

"You're gorgeous, Anika. You make me laugh, and you're kind, and you're so different from anyone else. You're the most beautiful girl I've ever seen, Anika."

My stomach twisted a little bit. It was a good answer; so why didn't I feel like it was? Because he mentioned my appearance twice, maybe?

He leaned down and kissed me slowly, but the sparks I'd felt yesterday weren't really there anymore. I was probably just tired from spending the day with Foster, but it bothered me. "I have my own birthday thing set up for you. We're gonna watch some movies and lie in your room for a while."

I nodded. "Okay. That sounds fun."

Brady pecked me on the lips one more time then led me upstairs.

But I didn't feel excited.

# Chapter 15

*Brady*

"Mom, stop. Yes, I thought about it. I don't know yet."

I listened quietly, not opening my eyes yet.

"Look, Washington sounds great, it does, but... no, this isn't about that... Mom!" Anika sounded irritated. "If you would just listen... yes, I—Mom. Mom. Listen. I've been thinking it over. If you just give me a little more time I'll... No, Mom. Don't put Dad on the...!" She paused. "Hey, Daddy. Yeah, I'm thinking. I know... I know... Yes... No, Dad, stop taking Mom's side on this."

A pause.

"Are you feeling better at least? I mean, the medicine, is it working?" continued Anika. She'd said her dad got sick recently. Judging by the way she exhaled, though, it didn't sound like good news. "It'll work. I know it will. Just take it when you're meant to, don't give Mom hell about going to the doctor all the time, and it'll be okay. As far as the house, though..."

What could she be arguing about with him?

"What do you mean? You're just gonna... you already did? But if I don't... yeah, I know, but... Dad, the college there is great, I know, but... No! I didn't just waste my high school career doing all of this for nothing, but college is two years away... Don't pull that card, you know I want to go to Washington State. Dad... Dad... No, Dad... Ugh! You're not listening!"

I sat up.

Anika's wide blue eyes shot to me. "Daddy, I have to go. No, don't— I'm hanging up. Bye, love you," she said hurriedly.

Suspicion pulled at my stomach. "You're moving?"

She shook her head slowly. "No… I don't want to yet."

"Anika, is that the college you want to go to?"

"Well, yes, but—"

"Your family is already there, aren't they?"

"Yeah, but—"

"Then go."

Her eyes widened a little bit. "What?"

"Go to Washington, Anika. You've spent weeks thinking about this. Four weeks ago, on your birthday, you told me that you weren't going to leave because you wanted to stay here with me and that you were going to tell your mom you weren't going." I trailed my gaze from her hair down her arm, then settled my gaze on her leg. "I want you to go to Washington. Your family is there, and the college you want to go to is there."

"I don't want to—"

"I want you to leave."

She stopped talking. "What?"

"I want you to leave," I repeated quietly. I'd been able to tell for about a week now that she was losing interest in me. She preferred working on homework over talking to me, and she'd only let me sleep over twice in the past month, not including the night I stayed over for her birthday. My chest hurt as I repeated my statement. I didn't want to let go of her. But she needed me to because she wasn't going to do it herself. As her interest had ebbed, mine had started to as well.

"Oh," she almost whispered.

I sat quietly for a moment. "I love you."

Anika's eyes teared up.

"You can't say it back." A small smile played on my lips. I knew she couldn't say it back to me. I'd known that when I said it. "That's okay. You don't need to love me."

A tear slipped down her cheek and she wiped it away quickly. "I'm sorry."

"Don't be."

God, this hurt. She was crying, I was losing her, and she was going to move to the other side of the country. I was breaking up with the girl I wanted. Pushing myself to my feet, I stopped at the door and smiled a little. *Someday, I'll be good enough for you, Anika. I promise.*

And I left.

***

*Anika*

"Yes. You should go, Anika," said Sierra.

I closed my eyes. Mitchell had told me to leave too.

"I want what's best for you, Anika. I always have, haven't I? You're my best friend. Even if we haven't spoken in a while, I do love you, and it's not like you won't be able to text me from Washington. Maybe you can even come visit during the summer. You'd be happier there, I think. Trust me on this, Anika. You need to go to Washington."

"What do you think I should do?" I'd hung up the phone with Mitchell an hour ago, and now I needed to ask Sierra.

"I think... you should stay. But that's being selfish, I think. Because I want you to stay so that I can keep you to myself, you know? You're so smart. You'll get into the college there if you want to, and you have the credits to graduate this year if you really try for it. As much as I want you to stay, I think you need to go."

I closed my eyes. "Okay."

***

*Mitchell*

I looked at the phone in my lap and smiled a little bit despite the tears burning my eyes. She was leaving. She was actually leaving; I mean, she'd been gone from me for a while now, but now she was actually physically leaving. I'd wanted to ask her to stay, but I couldn't force myself to do it. Anika needed to get away from everyone here. Foster. Brady. Sierra. She needed to get away from all of them.

So I couldn't ask her to stay with me.

Then again, her leaving didn't mean I wouldn't still see her.

***

### Sierra

I tapped the button on my phone to hang up and fell backward onto my bed. "Anika's leaving," I said quietly to myself. "She's moving to Washington, and I told her to do it." I closed my eyes. "When's she leaving?" I wondered out loud. "Maybe she'll throw a party or something for herself. A going away party. If she doesn't, I will. I have to." I exhaled slowly. "After all, she's my best friend."

***

### Foster

I looked down at Anika. She was standing in front of my door and looking down at her feet.

"Um... Foster..."

A half-smile tugged at the corner of my mouth. "I know, Anika."

She was leaving. She'd changed her mind, and she was going to move to Washington.

"I'm sorry. My... My mom..." Her voice trembled a little bit.

I reached out and pulled her against me, wrapping my arms around her and holding her quietly, resting my head on top of hers. "This isn't going to change anything, Anika. I'll come for you someday." Another small smile tugged at my lips. This didn't have

96

to be a sad thing if I didn't let it be. Her leaving was going to provide her with so many new opportunities. Not to mention, it would mean a break from all of the stress she'd been put through in the past couple of months.

"Did Brady tell you?" she asked from trembling lips against my chest.

No. I'd listened to her phone calls all day. She'd called so many people for their opinions, and they had all told her to move in with her family. "Yes," I murmured.

She shook harder in my arms.

My heart cracked as I felt her crying.

"No one wants me to stay," she whimpered quietly.

She thought that? She thought we all wanted her to leave for *our* sake? Anger flashed through my body, making my hands twitch. "Anika, none of us want you to leave. We want you to have the chance of leading a great life. Your family is in Washington, and there is an amazing college there that you could get into so easily if you wanted to." Of course, I already knew she wanted to go to college there. "I want you to stay more than almost anything; the only thing I want more than that is what's best for you." I pulled back a little and pressed my lips to her forehead.

Anika fell quiet and stopped shaking. She tilted her head back a little and made eye contact. My entire body responded to her blue depths looking into my eyes. "Foster?"

"Yes?" I managed.

She hesitated, but the question in her eyes was clear.

I leaned in and pressed my lips to hers.

# Chapter 16

*Brady*

I stared up at my ceiling blankly. That's all I'd been able to do since I had broken up with Anika two days ago. My phone buzzed and I lifted it numbly.

**are you coming to anika's going away party?**

The text message from Sierra made my stomach churn. No. I wasn't going to go. I couldn't.

**hey anika wants to know if youre coming to her party**

I ground my teeth together as Mitchell's text message popped up. No. I wasn't going.

**Anika wants you at her party today. Be there.**

My jaw clenched hard as Foster's name flashed across my screen.

No. I wasn't going.

I looked at the form in my hand thoughtfully. Maybe I shouldn't sign up yet. Maybe there was time.

Maybes didn't get anyone much of anything in life, though.

\*\*\*

*Anika*

I sat on my kitchen counter, swinging my legs a little. I'd stopped crying about everyone wanting me to leave after I'd spoken to Foster a couple days ago. Slowly, I raised my hand to my lips and brushed my fingers over them, remembering how it had felt to have Foster's lips against mine. My eyes closed involuntarily and I just sat there. There was nothing to think about at this point. I'd already decided, and I'd already been told to go by everyone I knew. I'd bought the plane ticket. There was nothing in my way now. Nothing to make me stay. I touched my lips for a moment longer then let my hand fall.

Maybe there was.

***

*Mitchell*

I leaned back against the couch and looked at Anika. She was sitting on the other couch, smiling and laughing with Sierra. They were talking about things they'd done over the years, and I could tell Sierra was trying not to cry. After five years of being her friend, I'd learned to recognize when she wanted to cry. Even though she was smiling, even though her eyes were lit up, even though she was laughing, she was sad.

Anika smiled at something Sierra said and looked at her watch. Immediately the smile was gone, and I looked at my phone for the time. It was time for her to leave. I stood up and hugged her, smiling at Anika encouragingly. "You're going to love it there, Anika," I murmured, turning my head to kiss her cheek gently.

Her fingers tightened in the fabric of my shirt and I felt her shake a little.

***

*Sierra*

I took a deep breath and smiled at Anika. "Alright. Time to go, I guess?"

She nodded. She'd only just managed to pry herself away from Mitchell, who had immediately fled into the backyard. I hugged her and smiled. When I looked up, Foster was watching us from the front

99

door, looking outside. He was leaning against the door frame casually but I could see the tense muscles of his arms bulging a little bit.

He really did love her, didn't he?

***

*Foster*

I wrapped my arms around Anika and held her against me, closing my eyes. This would be the last time for a long time that I got to hold her like this with me. There was no way for me to stop her, though, and this was a great opportunity for her. She really would be happier in Washington with her family; I was certain of it. Besides, her family needed her.

I would keep tabs on her while she was gone. I'd watch. Someone had to make sure she was safe.

Anika's fingers tightened on the fabric of my shirt and I smiled, pressing my lips to the top of her head. "I'm never going to be more than one phone call away from you, Anika. If you ever want to see me, just call me and I'll be there, I promise."

She nodded a little against my chest.

*I love you, Anika. I'll always be yours.*

***

*Brady*

I watched as Anika got in the car. I'd refused to go to the party, mostly because I couldn't say goodbye to her for a second time, but I'd shown up. Seeing her disappear into the car destroyed me. All I wanted at that moment was to get out of my car and beg her to stay for me, to stay with me and just promise me that she'd never leave me.

*If we meet again, Anika, I promise you I'll be a different man.*

100

*Foster*

I watched Anika drive away and smiled a little.

"Why are you smiling?" asked Sierra.

"She's going to be happier there."

Sierra nodded beside me and kicked the ground lightly. "That asshole didn't show up."

"Yes, he did."

"No, he didn't. Are you delusional?"

"He didn't come inside," I informed her, watching Brady's car drive away in the opposite direction, "but he couldn't keep himself from coming. It's not in his personality to give up like that. I'm pretty sure he watched us the whole time."

"And you didn't say anything?"

"There was nothing to say."

I felt her turn her eyes on me. "You seriously hate him, huh?"

"I don't dislike Brady," I explained, still watching as his car turned the corner. "In fact, I envy him for getting as close to Anika as he did. I can understand why he fell in love with her; I did, after all. A little competition never killed anyone." A real smile slid onto my face. "That's why I'm smiling. She's going to come back eventually, and I'll be waiting for her when she does. We both will, I think." Suddenly my memory of something I wanted to ask flooded into my mind again. "Excuse me."

I made my way to the backyard.

Mitchell was looking down at a rock, a half-smile on his face. "I decorated this with Anika in sixth grade."

I nodded, but I wasn't going to get distracted. "Are you ever going to tell me why you paid that guy to drug Anika at Brady's party? Or are you just going to keep pretending that I'm blind?" He didn't say anything and I shook my head a little. "It's rather insulting that you thought I wouldn't figure that out, Mitchell."

He remained silent.

"I would not have let you get any closer than that, Mitchell. It's a good thing you listened to my warning and stopped hanging around Anika. I'd say I appreciate you listening to me and telling Anika to go to Washington if you didn't owe that much to her."

"You're so clueless," he said suddenly, twirling something in his hand absently.

"Hm?"

"She was never yours. She was never Brady's. Since that day in fifth grade, Anika was mine."

I looked down at the rock Mitchell was looking at. *Mitchell and Anika <3* was written on it. I'd been able to tell from day one that he wasn't mentally stable. Despite everything Anika said, despite Mitchell's efforts, despite everyone's blindness, I'd seen through it. If anyone was dangerous, it was him. A small penguin pendant swung in his fingers.

He'd been the dangerous one all along.

# Chapter 17

*One Year Later.*

*Foster*

I looked across the lake without much interest. Life had been pretty boring since Anika left. She didn't text me as often as I would have liked, but I didn't want to push her out of fear that she would stop talking altogether.

She was starting to look at applications for jobs in Washington, and she was already working on her college submission form for the college she wanted to go to, even though it was only the late beginning of senior year. In the past month, I'd only talked to her once. We'd been on the phone together for about two hours, and I'd felt utterly defeated when she hung up. I'd considered going to Washington dozens of times after she left, and every time I just reminded myself that I was part of the reason she left in the first place.

If I closed my eyes for a moment, I could still feel the way her lips had felt against mine for the last time. She'd asked me to kiss her, not with words but with her eyes, and there had been so much *want* on her lips that I thought she was going to change her mind again and stay. But she hadn't changed her mind, and I couldn't do anything about that.

Mitchell had dropped off the map entirely. He switched schools, and the last time I had heard him mentioned was four months ago when Sierra told me that he wasn't replying to anything she sent him. He'd even gotten a new phone. I didn't bother hacking it; there was no way he was a danger to Anika right now, and he would find the virus quickly anyway. But I would have to find out about his whereabouts if she came back. That was the only way I could protect her from him.

Brady was on the honor roll by the end of junior year, and he was coming second to me in all of the testing sessions so far this year. I knew he was trying to prove something; whether it was to himself, or me, or Anika, I wasn't sure, but he had completely changed when she'd left. There were rumors going around about him, but I was almost certain that he wasn't the kind of man to do what they said he was going to do. He just wasn't made of the kind of material required.

Sierra... hadn't been doing quite as well. When Brady surpassed her grades, she seemed to completely give up on school. On the rare occasions I saw her at school, she never looked interested in anything. She was still the same annoyingly happy girl that she had been when Anika was here, but she wasn't trying anymore. For almost anything. Clearly, she was still proud of her appearance, but there was just no effort in anything else anymore, as far as I could tell. I didn't go out of my way to talk to her, but I did keep my eye on her for Anika's sake. She didn't have a job and she was failing almost half of her classes that she needed to pass. But that was none of my business; as long as she was physically okay, I didn't need to step in.

I still watched Anika's phone camera sometimes when I missed her, but she didn't spend nearly as much time on it as I would have hoped. Sometimes when I hacked her text messages, I would find pictures of some random guy in her inbox: Scott. The pictures never remained on her phone for more than fifteen seconds after she opened them. If he knew that, he might have taken the hint and left her alone.

Her music taste had shifted dramatically when she left. While I was looking through her iTunes account, I found songs like *What Hurts The Most* by Rascal Flatts and *Far Away* by Nickelback, purchased right after she left. Eventually, her spending habits went back to normal, but the number of plays for sad songs was still increasing, even now. I wondered idly if she missed me at all. It was okay if she didn't. She didn't have to love me yet. One day, she would come to love me of her own accord, and I would be waiting for her when she did.

Despite knowing she would come back, doubt still gnawed at my mind every day. Every day, I was pulled back down into the dark, depressing realization that she really wasn't here anymore. That I wasn't going to go to school and see her. That it had been over a full year since she left. At one point, about six months after her leaving, I'd found myself thinking darker thoughts than usual.

I'd leveled out drastically since she'd left, though. I reminded myself of who she was and that I didn't need to be "creepy," as she put it, and that there were more ways to show her my love than just watching her cameras and checking up on her. If she came back, I would get rid of all of the cameras. That much was certain.

The few times I had talked to her since her departure were so amazing. Hearing her voice was like taking a deep breath of fresh air after being held underwater for minutes at a time; every time I was certain that I was going to drown, she was there again. Like she could feel me losing my grip, even though she was so far away.

Water splashed onto my foot and I looked at it thoughtfully. That's exactly how I could explain what I felt: drowning.

The slow suffocation from not being able to talk to her, the inability to do anything to pull myself away from the situation. I was drowning. But, as I said before, she kept saving me, and every time she did, I was so grateful that I would be okay for longer periods of time.

Someday I would tell her about this. About how I felt when she wasn't with me. About how everyone who had depended on her changed so dramatically. She had no idea how much she had affected their lives. Someday we would look back on this together with happiness rather than sadness because it had only strengthened us to find out that we could keep our feelings alive despite the distance.

Someday I was going to go get her and bring her back. Or maybe I'd stay with her instead.

My phone buzzed and my heart pounded anxiously like it did every time my text tone went off; every time, I hoped it was Anika.

**foster?**

**yes?** I replied, without hesitation.
**can you come to washington?**

# Chapter 18

I bounced my leg nervously as I sat on the bench. My plane had landed only minutes ago but I was so impatient to see Anika that it felt like years since I'd landed in Washington. Her name was racing through my head; no, through my veins. It consumed me, and the mental picture of her was making me even more impatient. It hadn't even occurred to me to check her phone. Maybe I should, I thought. Could she have gotten stuck somewhere? Could she see me from where she was? Maybe she wasn't coming at all…?

Then I saw her.

She looked so different. Her brown hair was cut so short that it looked like a pixie cut, but it was beautiful on her. Her body looked so much more… toned. She'd mentioned getting really into running since she'd been in Washington and it was very clear now. Anika was still a delicate beauty, with the gentle curves of her face and the soft cream color of her skin, but there was something almost dangerous about her now with her newly muscled legs. She wore a tank top and jeans, and I didn't even register getting up before I had my arms around her, pulling her to my chest.

A vanilla coconut scent flooded my nose and swirled around me; it was intoxicating.

"Foster, I can't breathe."

Her voice was amused but I loosened my grip on her. I wasn't ready to let go of her just yet. I wanted to stay like this for hours, despite the crowded airport moving around us.

I pulled back a little to look at her. To study her face. I'd missed looking into those sapphire labyrinths.

She looked… tired. Happy, but tired. I pulled her against my chest again and closed my eyes. I'd missed her so much. Every desire I'd had to feel her was finally being relieved, with my arms around her waist pulling her to me so tightly.

A boy chuckled and I looked up.

It was the boy from the pictures on her phone.

Scott.

He had sandy blond hair and warm hazel eyes, and a huge grin was spread across his face. "You're Foster, I guess?"

Immediately my hostility went up and I tightened my grip on Anika. "Yes."

"Nice to meet you." He flashed another smile, but I was irritated.

Anika felt me tense up and sighed quietly. "Old habits die hard, I guess." She pushed on my chest a little and pointed. "This is Scott, my *friend*." The emphasis she put on *friend* was clearly directed at me, and it didn't seem to bother him at all; his smile didn't falter. So they weren't together, then? Her bright blue eyes were happy; she didn't seem to have any hurt feelings attached to him. So it was mutual, then. She saw the hostility drain from my eyes and hugged me tightly. "I missed you, Foster."

I'd been waiting for those words for so long.

All I wanted to do was kiss her.

"C'mon, we're gonna go back to my house," she said.

"I thought I was staying in a hotel?"

"No, we have a couple extra rooms now. My dad's mechanic shop got some insane donation from an anonymous person and now he's making, like, three times what he was making before, even though he can't work much now." She smiled at me again, flashing her white teeth.

A small smile threatened to reveal my thoughts, but I suppressed it. There was no reason to ruin the anonymity. "Alright, let's go."

*\*\*\**

I nodded as I approached the house. "Very nice house."

108

Anika laughed. "You practically live in a mansion and you think this is nice?"

I chuckled in response and looked at her. She'd changed; it was a good change, though, and I could adapt to it. The normal sarcastic tone that lightened her voice wasn't there anymore and the aggressive nature appeared to have completely left her. Maybe her running had helped her to calm down and mellow out? I could handle that, though. However she'd changed, I could accept it and adapt to it. She was still Anika. I still loved her.

"These bags are so hard to carry," said Scott.

Scott's voice irritated me a little. I'd asked to carry my own stuff but he'd insisted that he carry it, and now he was complaining. The entire ride over here he'd been making really stupid puns and referencing movies and TV shows I'd never seen before. If I had understood the references it might have been bearable, but it was ridiculous. Who the hell had seen *Sharknado*? What the hell was that? What Anika saw in him was completely over my head. If she could be interested in someone like me, how could she also be interested in someone like… *him*?

"Hey, I'm gonna throw these in a guest room and go talk to your dad, alright?" said Scott.

Anika nodded in reply then turned to face me once we were alone again. "So." She smiled. "Anything interesting happen while I was gone?"

"I'm pretty sure nothing interesting is *capable* of happening when you're gone, Anika." My voice came out a little huskier than I had intended it to, rough with emotion. I meant it; nothing major happened since she left, other than Mitchell's apparent disappearance. I was so relieved to be with her that I couldn't control my voice. I looked around the room. "There's pictures of your family in this room. You didn't have pictures at your last house."

She tilted her head. "Yeah. We never saw the point in pictures. That is, until Charlie came onto the scene."

"Who's Charlie?"

"The little sister I didn't know I had. Well, half-sister, I guess." Anika's voice trailed a little as she looked around the room. "My mom was out of our lives for about a year a couple of years back, and I guess this is why. She's back now though, and Charlie's apparently been living with her dad until now. He got arrested or something. She's been with us for..." she exhaled slowly as she thought, "two months now? I don't know exactly. All of the time recently has blurred together." Her blue eyes shone as she looked at me. "She's sweet, though. I've always wanted a sister."

I smiled. As long as this wasn't bothering her, it was a good thing, right? My gaze slid along the pictures, looking for the little girl. When I found her, I was surprised; she was only a couple of years old. Her blue eyes matched Anika's and she had brown hair, but the shade of brown was more dirty blonde. Cute kid. I wondered vaguely if my own mother had had more children since she left us.

"Do you want to meet her? She's with my dad right now, I think. My mom's really pushing for them to be close," said Anika.

I nodded. "I'd love to."

She smiled at me and led me to a door which I found out led to the kitchen.

I saw three things in this room.

Anika's father.

Charlie.

And Mitchell.

# Chapter 19

*Foster*

*Six Years Ago*

I wiped my palms on my dress pants nervously as I looked around the lunch room. Middle school was so... intimidating. Maybe I wasn't ready for public school. Maybe I should call my dad to come get me. Maybe... Maybe no one would ever like me. There wasn't much to like anyway, and in the two months at this school, no one had tried to talk to me unless they needed help with homework. I just wanted one friend, and that would be enough. Everyone that knew who my dad was treated me badly. No one wanted to talk to me.

I took a deep breath. Today was the day I tried to sit with the other kids.

My eyes slid skittishly across the tables. Where would I sit? There were so many people... Who was I to even think any of them *wanted* me to sit with them? Finally, I saw a kid from my art class. His name was Brady. Maybe... Maybe he would let me sit with him. He seemed nice, kind of. His art was okay when he wasn't looking at a girl the whole time. In his defense, she was beautiful. So beautiful that I'd dropped a paint palette on my pants when she asked to borrow it. Girls were difficult to deal with. Especially that one. She seemed kind of mean sometimes, and she would only talk to two people. That wasn't fair. I wanted to talk to her, but... How? She was the kind of girl that you wanted to impress when you talked to her for the first time; that wasn't my skill set. She had spoken to me a few times, and she always said really nice things, but I had nothing to impress her with. All I was good at was computers. What kind of girl likes that?

I looked at Brady nervously when I reached the table. "U-um... Brady... is... is it okay if I um... could I maybe sit... with you?"

Brady looked at me with a confused expression. "Do I know you?"

"I... I'm in your..." My palms were sweaty and I shook my head quickly. "N-nothing, I'm sorry, I-I'll go."

As I turned my back, they started laughing at me. Tears filled my eyes and I clenched my fists as I fled. Why had I even asked? I wasn't cool or athletic or strong like them. I was just a short kid with messy hair and neon braces; I could barely lift my textbooks. I was a total wimp.

*** 

I sat on the swing and looked at the ground as tears rolled off my cheeks and fell into the mulch of the school playground, disappearing as if they'd never existed.

"Are you crying?" asked a boy.

I looked up and wiped my cheeks. "N-no," I managed between hiccups.

"You totally are, you baby." The boy grinned evilly at me and laughed.

I looked up at him and stood up. He was my age, but he was so much taller. I'd always been a short kid. "Leave me alone."

He grinned again and shoved my shoulder so I fell.

The swing went out from under me, sending me sprawling to the ground. My head hit the ground hard and I stared up at the boy in fear. "S-stop it! Leave me alone!"

"Make me, crybaby! You think you're cool because your dad is rich but you aren't! You're just ugly and short and nerdy!"

"Knock that off." A few feet away stood the beautiful girl with brown hair from my art class. Anika. She looked at the boy uncertainly, while another boy tugged at her arm, begging for them to leave.

The nasty boy walked toward the girl quickly and shoved her by the shoulders. "Wanna make me?"

She stumbled backward and stared at the boy but changed her stance and turned her entire body to face him. "Yeah, I do!"

He glared at her. "Stupid girl." The boy shoved her harder and this time she fell down.

I stared. What was she doing?

Anika winced but pushed herself to her feet again. "Leave him alone."

This time, when he shoved her to the ground, he stepped on her stomach and she half screamed, starting to struggle. What could I do? Why did she stand up? Why was she helping me?

The boy who had been with Anika came running back, towing a tiny blonde with him and the girl held up a whistle. "I-I'll blow this whistle if you don't stop and you'll get expelled because the teachers put me in charge of the anti-bullying club!" she squeaked nervously, clearly uncertain of what she was saying.

I watched the boy get off of her with a roll of his eyes and run off after glaring at me again. I lay on the ground just staring at her. Why had she…?

"Are you okay?" she muttered quietly in my direction.

I nodded slowly. "Th-thank you."

Then she did something that confused me.

She smiled.

I kept staring.

"I'm glad you're okay. I didn't want to watch someone get hurt. Especially someone so small. You need to be protected."

I nodded slowly again.

She offered me her hand and helped me up. The blonde with the whistle stood off to the side with the other boy that I'd seen and I looked up at her in confusion.

"I think people should protect people more often instead of fighting," she murmured, not looking at me directly. "The world would be better."

"A-aren't..." I tried desperately to find my voice, "aren't boys meant to be the ones protecting the girls?"

She thought for a moment. "Nah. I don't think so." For the first time, she looked me dead in the eyes. "I think people should protect the people they feel need protecting, no matter what." Anika looked away a little again. "That's all."

A bell rang.

"Lunch is over. Bye!" She grabbed the other boy by the hand and ran off to the school with him and the girl.

***

I poked my food without interest.

My dad looked at me and raised an eyebrow. "Is something wrong, Foster?"

I clenched my teeth. Yesterday at school, I found out Brady beat up the boy that hurt me and Anika on Monday. He protected her. He did something about it. Why hadn't I? Why was I such a wimp? Why was I so small? Why... Why hadn't I done anything when she got hurt by him? I should have... helped her. *Protected* her. It was a boy's job, even if she said it wasn't. "Dad, I don't like my school. I want to go somewhere else where there aren't any bullies."

He was quiet for a moment. "What do you say we go to our house in Alaska until you're ready to come back and face whatever you're running from?"

I nodded and looked down at my dinner. "Dad, how do you protect someone?"

He chuckled. "Sometimes you can't protect people from everything. The only way you could keep someone safe all the time is if you watched them on a camera or something," he laughed again, louder, "but that isn't a realistic way to deal with anything."

I nodded. "Let's go to Alaska."

He nodded distantly. "I'll have the plane here in the morning."

Finally, I took a bite of spinach, something that made my dad stare at me in surprise. I never ate vegetables. But if I was going to be big enough to protect people, to not get pushed around by anyone anymore, I needed to change.

I wouldn't be helpless next time.

Never again.

# Chapter 20

*Anika*

I glared up at Foster as he looked away like nothing had happened. He was looking at the walls of my room, holding one of his smaller suitcases carelessly.

"You can't put me in timeout," he muttered, pouting.

"Actually, I can. If Daddy hadn't gotten between you and Mitchell, you could have hurt him. Ugh, I thought you would have gotten over this by now. You can't just kill all of my friends, Foster!" I took a deep breath and exhaled slowly. "Seriously, if you try to hurt him again, you can't stay here. I invited you because I truly missed you, and you're trying to kill my best friend within twenty minutes."

Foster's eyes shot to mine immediately, their black depths flickering. "You'd let him stay but not me?"

There was a knock on my door and I turned to look at Mitchell, who was shifting awkwardly from foot to foot.

I sighed. "Come in."

Mitchell stood a few feet away from Foster and me. "If it's really a problem, I could leave, Anika. I don't want to make anyone uncomfortable."

I reached out and took his hand reassuringly. "No. You're my best friend, and you were here first. You've already been staying with us for a couple weeks. I'm not making you leave just because Foster can't behave."

When I looked at Foster, his face had paled and he was looking at my hand in Mitchell's with burning hate.

116

I released Mitchell's hand gently. "Go help Daddy finish making dinner. Foster and I have some rules to discuss."

Mitchell smiled at me and nodded, going back into the hall toward the kitchen.

"Rules?" Foster repeated.

"Rule one, you can't attack anyone that stays here or visits me. Manslaughter is rude. Rule two, don't do anything creepy in front of my parents; I'd say 'at all' but I'm pretty sure you haven't changed that much based off of what I just saw. Rule three, you have to apologize to Mitchell. Rule four. My graduation party is in seven days; you have to leave within ten days, okay? There's going to be about seventy people at the party, maybe more. I invited you here so you could come to the party. I didn't know you'd be willing to come so soon."

"Senior year isn't even half over."

"Mitchell graduated early and suggested I do the same thing. We both have enough credits to go to college, and he's going to Washington State too, so I figured there's no point in wasting the rest of the year at this school. Now, agree to my rules."

He sighed and nodded. "Fine, whatever you want, Anika." His tone made me wonder what else he was thinking about.

The way he said my name gave me slight chills and my face felt a little warm. I hadn't heard his voice in so long that I'd almost forgotten what it was like. The same deep, smooth tone it had had a year ago was present now, but he sounded calmer. Maybe he had changed.

"I like the way you smell, by the way. I noticed it at the airport."

Ah, there was the creepy Foster I knew.

***

*Foster*

I waited semi-patiently for Mitchell. Anika had insisted I apologize to him before dinner. Fury still pricked my gut. He had been here for weeks. He was going to college with her. He had convinced her to

117

leave high school to spend more time with him. He was so much smarter than I had given him credit for. But that could come later; I had other matters to deal with right now. My eyes skimmed her room slowly now. Technically, I wasn't meant to be in here anymore, but I needed to install my cameras. If Mitchell was coming in here at night, I needed to know about it.

I looked behind me for a moment at the door, then picked up a bell I found on Anika's dresser and tied it to the knob before shoving a shirt under the door. The bell would signal if anyone was there and the shirt would provide me with just enough time to retreat thanks to the resistance it would create.

I unlocked my suitcase and pulled out several sizes of cameras, judging which one would fit best in the vent above her window. Finally, I decided on a medium one and turned on the wireless camera, then checked the battery life. I knew it would last for seven days of filming before I had to change the batteries if untouched. Perfect.

I pulled out a screwdriver and hummed quietly to myself as I undid the screws of the vent. *I see trees of green, red roses too, hmmm hmm hmmm hmmmmm, for me and you, and I think to myself, what a wonderful world...* Sure, I didn't know all the words, but it was still a good song.

*Finally.* The vent screws fell easily into the palm of my hand and I looked inside.

My stomach dropped.

There was already a camera there.

The tiny bell went off and I shoved the screws back into the holes of the vent desperately. Anika had almost caught me installing cameras in her room once before at her last house, and my heart was beating wildly at the idea of her catching me this time. I threw my screwdriver under her bed and shoved the camera into my pocket before snapping shut my suitcase and going to the door, removing the shirt.

Mitchell looked up at me with a subtly suspicious expression.

I looked back at him unhappily. "Anika is a bit messy, I guess."

118

"Yes," he agreed slowly. Mitchell's eyes skimmed the room thoroughly as he spoke. He was looking to see what I had been doing. "Anika said you were ready to apologize to me."

Irritation choked my voice and I glared at him hatefully. If I got the chance, I would hurt him, badly. "Yes. Can we just pretend I apologized?"

A small smirk spread across his face. "It would be more satisfying if I heard you say it."

My jaw clenched furiously and my hands twitched. "I'm sorry," I snarled.

He smiled at me brightly. "All is forgiven."

Mitchell turned his back on me so that he could leave and I contemplated just shoving him so that his face hit the opposite wall of the hallway. Seeing blood pour from his face would make me feel better. Seeing it happen because of me would make me feel twice as good about it happening. But he would tell Anika. And I couldn't leave while she was in danger.

"Oh, and Foster?" said Mitchell. "I am not afraid of you anymore. Remember that." And, with a smile, he disappeared from my view.

# Chapter 21

*Anika*

I licked my spoon lazily and swung my legs as I sat on the kitchen counter with my ice cream. It had been months since I could sleep properly; maybe even a year. My eyes closed as I thought about my old house. The nights I spent with Mitchell, telling ghost stories until we fell asleep. The nights I spent with Brady, the first boy I'd slept with whom I'd felt something vaguely romantic for. Swirling my ice cream, I let my tired eyes close.

"You're up pretty late."

Chills spread slowly over my skin. "You're up pretty early, Foster. It's four in the morning." I opened my eyes to look at the black-haired boy in my kitchen. His pajama pants hung loosely on his hips, and he wasn't wearing a shirt. I'd never really realized how pale his skin was until now. Heat spread through my cheeks as my eyes traveled down his chest to his V-line dipping below my line of sight. Was this the first time I was seeing him shirtless? My cheeks heated up again and I averted my eyes politely from his naked torso and looked out of the patio door.

"You can look," he murmured quietly. I heard him walking toward me and when I looked at him again, he was close enough for me to touch him.

I looked at him for a moment, trying to decipher his facial expression, but his dark eyes gave nothing away.

Slowly and hesitantly, Foster reached out and brushed my hair away from my face. Heat burned me pleasantly where his fingers touched. Pink tinged his cheeks and he looked away, letting his hand fall. "I like your haircut. I didn't get the chance to say that yet." His eyes made their way to mine again and his always intense gaze made me unable to move.

"Thanks. I like it too. It's a lot easier to manage this way."

"I'll miss your messy bun style, though. And I'll also miss the shampoo you used to use. It was very pleasant and matched your body wash. Now you mix them and it's a bit more distracting for me."

I sighed quietly. Creepy Foster was back again.

Foster's eyes trailed down to the bowl of ice cream in my hands. "Six days until your party," he said quietly. "Nine days until I have to leave."

I nodded.

"Ten days with you isn't enough," added Foster.

"You have to go home though, Foster. School, you probably have a job, your dad lives there—"

"You called it home even though you don't live there anymore. Why?"

I hesitated, thinking about my answer carefully. "I miss it. You're there, and Mitchell technically lives there still, and Sierra, and…" I shook my head, the last name not daring to roll off my tongue. I hadn't said his name once since I had moved. I couldn't. I hadn't even been able to call him to ask him to come to my graduation party; I wasn't sure what I would do if I saw him. "My life is there, you know? That makes it home to me."

"You can always come back, whenever you want," he murmured. "I could pay for your plane ticket if you want. You could stay at my house, and you could see Sierra every day if you wanted."

I stayed quiet.

Foster's hand touched the hand I was using to hold the counter, making me refocus my eyes on him. "Please, think about it," said Foster. "When I leave, I'm not sure I can go another year with minimal contact. It's… It was so… *difficult* for me not to come here before you said I could."

"Foster…" I wasn't sure what to say to him. What *could* I say?

His eyes bored into mine and he inched a little closer, almost touching his body to the counter, mere inches from where I was sitting. My heart sped up a little and I watched his eyes flicker just below my eyes. I bit my lip a little self-consciously. He noticed and his eyes darkened a little. "Don't tempt me like that," Foster half groaned, half growled. He closed his eyes and stood there for a moment before pushing himself away from the counter with slight force, looking into my eyes again. "I'm going to sleep for a few more hours, alright?"

I nodded slowly and my entire body relaxed.

Foster walked out of the kitchen and I watched the door for a moment after he closed it.

Finally, I exhaled. I hadn't even realized I had been holding my breath when he had gotten so close to me. Or rather, that I had stopped breathing. I spooned another small mouthful of ice cream into my mouth and after putting the bowl in the sink, I stepped down from the counter and walked out into my living room. The time was starting to get to me, and exhaustion begged my body to go back to bed. The familiar irritability that came with mornings was beginning to tinge my mood and I started making my way to my room.

There was a slight knocking sound and I turned around in confusion at the bottom of the stairs.

The knock came again and I almost yelped in surprise. I'd seen *Paranormal Activity*. Every time the girl checked out the weird noise, she died. I considered calling for Foster; the smart, big ones lived sometimes. Slowly, I walked toward the door. If I was attacked by a serial killer, I was pretty sure I could scream in time for Foster to come help before I was stabbed to death.

Okay, deep breaths. Just open the door. It wasn't that hard, right? I'd opened tons of doors. Not for serial killers but hey, gotta try new things, right? New experiences built character. Death, but also character.

The knock came a third time as I reached the door and I opened it slowly, poking my head around the door. A large black figure appeared as I opened it all the way. My pulse hammered hard.

The figure grabbed me tightly and I screamed loudly, half struggling against the strong arms around me.

Almost immediately, footsteps raced into the living room, and the light flicked on. I stared up at who had grabbed me and my eyes widened at the person with his arms around me.

"Brady."

# Chapter 22

*Foster*

I stared blankly as Brady's familiar frame appeared in the light of the living room. I'd come rushing into the room when Anika screamed, and both her father and Mitchell were in the room now too. Brady grinned down at a very clearly surprised Anika.

"Hi to you too."

She stared at him and we all waited to see what she would do next. Finally, she wrapped her arms around him and clung to him. Anger and jealously flooded my veins and I wanted to break his arms. "Why in the world are you here?" asked Anika. "I didn't invite you. How the hell did you even get my address? Why are you here at four in the morning?"

Brady chuckled and his hand ran down her back slowly, up and down. "Well—"

A small blonde wove her way around Brady and squealed, launching herself at Anika and immediately stealing her away from Brady, squeezing her hard enough that she squeaked in surprise at the new person's grip. "I missed you!" Sierra squealed.

Anika laughed and hugged her tiny friend. "Of course it's you. You always make an entrance."

Once the greetings were over, I stood awkwardly off to the side, watching. Sierra walked to Mitchell and hugged him too, and Anika's father shook hands with Brady.

"So, um, Anika, I know you didn't invite Brady but I thought I should bring him anyway, and since it was a surprise I didn't want to bring this up on the phone, but—"

No.

Do not say it.

"—is it okay if he stays here too?"

No.

It isn't.

"Of course." Anika smiled at Sierra but I saw hesitation behind her eyes. Was she still upset about the way they had parted? Did she feel uncomfortable with him being here now that the excitement had ebbed enough for her to realize what was going on? I would have given anything to know what was going on in her head when she saw him.

Brady's eyes finally found me and he looked at me without much interest. "Foster's here." His tone was flat and full of distaste. I didn't care.

"All of this is very exciting," Anika's father, Jensen, started, "but it's a very terrible hour of the night to have five teenagers giving me a headache. Could we postpone this to tomorrow?"

Anika rolled her eyes a little but sighed and nodded. "Yeah, good idea." She hesitated. "I don't have a room ready for Brady."

Brady smirked teasingly. "I could sleep with you."

Immediately, Anika's father raised his hand. "Hello? Dad in the room. Could you not make me think about the fact that my daughter is now in a house with three teenage boys more than I have to?"

I chuckled quietly. A flash caught my attention. Mitchell was taking pictures again. My eyes narrowed at him but he wasn't watching me. He was watching Anika.

And from a few feet away, with painfully ecstatic eyes, so was Brady.

\*\*\*

I yawned when I opened my eyes and sat up slowly, stretching. I'd only been asleep for a few hours since Brady and Sierra arrived, and I could smell bacon and coffee downstairs. I took a moment to consider this.

At Anika's other house, it was cold and quiet and smelled only like her. Here, it was warm and full of laughter and smelled like coffee all the time. Here, she had a home. It had been the right choice to tell her to move here. Though I still hadn't seen her mother, I was certain this house had a much more "family" vibe than the other one. Knowing this made my year of mind-numbing boredom and sadness worth it; she'd been happy the whole time, and that was what mattered.

I pushed myself to my feet and walked to the kitchen. Anika was nibbling on the corner of a Pop-Tart, Sierra was cooing over Charlie and giving her pieces of banana, and Jensen was sipping coffee, leaning against the counter and watching Anika and Sierra with affectionate eyes.

Sierra grinned at Charlie. "You like bananas? Yes, yes we do," she cooed and grinned, putting a small piece of banana into the toddler's mouth.

Anika looked up irritably at Sierra. "Vampire in the room, Could we avoid all of the morning energy, please? Also, Dad, could you make me some bacon, please?"

"Sure. Sierra, you want any?"

Sierra wrinkled her nose. "I'm a vegetarian now. I'll pass."

"Bacon is a vegetable. Pigs eat grass. So really, bacon is just converted grass. Chocolate is a vegetable too, by the way because, blah blah, something about cocoa beans."

Sierra laughed. "You would make a terrible vegan."

Mitchell walked past me and sat next to Anika, chuckling.

She groaned quietly and mumbled about mornings and bacon under her breath before leaning her head on Mitchell's shoulder. He stroked her hair slowly and looked up at me. The gleam in his eyes was infuriating. He *wanted* to provoke me.

Reality hit me like a bus. If I lost control, I would have to leave. If I left, she would be unprotected.

Mitchell smiled at me innocently then kissed Anika's forehead. "I'm gonna go grab everyone some coffee. Do you want anything?"

Anika nodded. "Alcohol."

Jensen snorted from across the kitchen.

Mitchell flicked her ear and she winced. "No drinking, missy."

"I'm going to be old enough in two years," she muttered. "I'm an adult, you know."

"No, you're a child, and in two years you'll be a child with a drinking permit. What kind of coffee do you want?"

"I want a venti French vanilla espresso with two shots of caramel, one shot of almond, no fat, soy milk only, two sugar packets, and one inch of foam," Sierra piped up.

"Would it be wrong to slap her for being so stereotypically white?" Anika growled as she let her head hit the table. "Is there any chance you know what I want?"

Mitchell smiled and nodded. "Of course. You always get a black coffee with caramel in it, then add vanilla creamer when you get it. I'll be back in a little while. Jensen, I'll get you your regular too."

Jensen glared half-heartedly. "I already made coffee."

"And as soon as you figure out how to work a filter so I don't have to chew my coffee, I'll drink it." Mitchell grinned.

Jensen waved his hand dismissively as if to shoo Mitchell. "You kids have no taste nowadays. Go on then."

I stood there silently. Mitchell passed me and I turned to face Anika. "I'm going to take a shower. Anika, would you mind if I used the bathroom connected to your room? I believe Brady is in the other one."

She groaned.

Sierra giggled. "That's Morning Anika's way of saying yes."

I nodded and walked up the stairs to Anika's room, closing the door behind me. Immediately I went to the vent to check for the camera. As I used the multitool in my pocket to unscrew the vent, I felt like I was being watched. Then again, maybe that was just the sensation I was getting from the camera lodged in the vent. Then a voice came from the doorway.

"What are you doing?"

# Chapter 23

*Brady*

*Six Months Ago*

I looked up at Anika's house. Sometimes I would walk by here when I had nothing better to do or when I missed her. No one had moved in here yet; it was like the house was waiting for her to come back, just like I was. It felt like time had stopped when she left. Nothing happened anymore. I stopped going to football practice, stopped partying. I'd sworn that I would be good enough for her the night she drove away from me, and I was going to do it. Every day since she left, I had strived to be the best I could possibly be, and I still wasn't sure it was enough.

Maybe I never would be.

But the papers sitting in my room would give me a chance to do something good with my life. Whether it was or wasn't for Anika anymore, I was a better man, and I liked who I was now. I didn't make out with every girl who asked, or throw parties every weekend, or drink, or sneak out at night. Even if Anika wasn't part of my future, at least I had one now.

\*\*\*

*Three Months Ago*

Sierra's high-pitched voice was starting to get on my nerves; I was trying to study. I only really kept her around because she reminded me of Anika. It was painful sometimes to go too long without the slightest reminder of her; I could see Foster was suffering too when I saw him. It always made me angry to see him like that. He was the one who would never deserve her. Yet here he was, acting like he was the one that dated her.

Like he was the one who meant something to her.

Like he was the one who had fallen in love with her.

I loved Anika. He didn't. My pencil snapped in my hand and I looked down at it, mildly surprised.

"You thinking about Anika again?" Sierra asked gently, her bright eyes glittering with concern.

I gritted my teeth.

"She *did* care about you, Brady."

"She hasn't talked to me once." My voice shook with emotion. Sometimes I got upset again over Anika, while other times I felt absolutely nothing toward the subject matter. I was starting to heal, I think. That's what it was when the pain lessened, right? "She left, and she hasn't spoken to me since." Pain seared through my chest and I tried my best to force it away, but I tried to remind myself of how much it had hurt before I'd gotten this close to being over her. If she had loved me, she would have stayed. Then again, I loved her, and I was the one who told her to leave. I'd given up on her, not the other way around. I should've been happy that she listened to me and left like that. But I wasn't. "Does... she ever mention me to you?"

Sierra hesitated. "I bring you up."

"And?"

"And... she changes the topic." Sierra's eyes caught mine and softened sadly. "I'm sorry, Brady. I know you two loved each other, but... she..." She sighed a little bit as she mentioned her best friend. "She's a complicated person, Brady. I can't tell what she's doing or what she's thinking, almost ever, and I'm the person who knows her better than anyone else, so I think that says something."

I nodded, clenching my jaw, and looked back down at my homework. "Let's just focus."

"Yeah," she murmured.

***

*Three Days Ago*

I looked at the yearbook from last year slowly, flipping through all of the pages until I came to her picture. My finger trailed over the page as I tried to will myself to turn it, but I couldn't. My eyes studied her face. I'd watched her face every time I saw her; in school, at night when we were together... and I'd never appreciated seeing it like I should have. I took it for granted that I could go to school every day and see her whenever I wanted.

A knock at my bedroom door caught my attention but I kept my eyes on Anika's picture. "What, Mom?"

The door opened. "Not quite."

I lifted my head at Sierra's voice and looked at her without much interest. "Why are you here?"

"I... well, I have something kind of weird to ask you."

"Spit it out, I'm busy."

She hesitated for a moment then threw something at me.

I caught it, and looked down at the paper in my hands, blinking slowly, trying to comprehend the words on the page. "You're invited to Anika Mason's graduation party," I read aloud in a flat voice. I noticed Sierra's name on the card and I raised my eyes to hers. "Why are you showing this to me? It's not for me."

"Well... My mom doesn't want me to travel alone." She fidgeted a little. "And Mitchell already left to go there."

"Spit it out, Sierra."

"I want you to come with me. You know, since in a few months you'll be—"

***

*4:09 in the morning*

131

I looked at the door hesitantly.

"C'mon, just knock already!" Sierra hissed behind me.

"It's four in the morning, Sierra, what are the chances she'll answer?"

"Trust me, she'll answer."

I took a deep, slightly shaky breath, and knocked on the door. After a moment, I knocked again. Then, excitement urged me to knock for a third time and the door opened slowly. A familiar face appeared. My eyes were well adjusted to the dark at this point and I could see the uncertain expression crossing her beautiful face that I had missed so intensely. My heart pounded wildly as I saw her and I lurched forward suddenly before I realized what I was doing and hugged her.

She screamed and I buried my face in her hair, hugging her slim body to mine. I'd missed this. I could do without the screaming part, though.

The lights came on and I heard multiple sets of footsteps rush into the room.

"Brady."

The way my name rolled off of her tongue gave me chills. I'd wanted this—needed this—for so long now. To just feel her with me again, her warmth against mine, her smooth hair in my face. It was so much shorter now. Her arms went around my waist suddenly and I closed my eyes, stroking her back slowly. I needed this so badly. "Hi to you too," I murmured. I needed to touch her; I needed to be sure she was really there. I'd been so close to being over her, but now that I had her in my arms again, leaving was the last thing I wanted to do. I wanted to touch her and hold her and kiss her again like I had before.

"Why in the world are you here? I didn't invite you. How the hell did you even get my address? Why are you here at four in the morning?"

I chuckled at the shocked tone of her voice and smiled, "Well—"

Suddenly Anika was torn from my arms by a squealing Sierra. Evidently she couldn't wait any longer than I could to hug her best friend. I watched her and Sierra as they talked. Their voices didn't even register in my mind above the joy I felt. Finally I tore my gaze from her to the other people in the room. My eyes landed on a tall muscular figure with black hair and my eyes narrowed. "Foster's here."

He was here. She had invited him, and she hadn't invited me.

Him.

Again.

***

Present

"What are you doing?"

I looked up the stairs toward Mitchell's voice and jogged to where he was standing in a doorway. Mitchell looked at me and nodded.

"What's going on?" I asked cautiously.

"Foster apparently didn't tell me that Anika said he could go into her room to fix her vent. I came to give him his screwdriver, but somehow he got it off on his own." Mitchell tilted his head and tossed the screwdriver into the room. I looked at the camera in his hand.

"Are you making a home improvement movie or something?"

He laughed. "No. I document everything that happens. I was just about to set this up in my room. I think someone was going through my things." Mitchell's eyes traveled back to the room. "I really don't like it when people mess with my stuff; I have very expensive cameras with me and if they were tampered with or moved, I'd be pretty upset about it. Anyway," he said, walking toward me, "I was just about to go get some coffee for everyone. Do you want anything?"

I shook my head. "Nah, man, coffee is for girls."

"What does that say about me?"

I smirked a little. "Do you want a real answer to that?"

Mitchell laughed good-naturedly and rolled his eyes. "I'm leaving. See you later." He moved past me and I walked to Anika's room, looking in at Foster. "You're fixing the vent?"

Foster was staring at the wall just beside the door and his arms were tense.

"The hell is wrong with you?" I asked.

His jaw was clenched. "Nothing," he growled slowly.

There really was no changing people who were creepy by nature. I shook my head and walked back down the stairs, into the kitchen and looked at Anika. "Is she dead? Should I poke her with something?"

"You will not be poking my daughter with anything."

I felt my face heat up though cold fear shot through my body at his voice; I hadn't realized her dad was in the room. "Not quite what I meant, sir."

We all sat in comfortable silence for about twenty minutes before something started to bother me. I'd been watching Anika happily as she laid her head on the table, looking half alive. I missed watching her wake up and be like this in the morning. "What's wrong with your vent? I thought your dad was a mechanic or something. Can't you have him fix it?" I looked at Anika questioningly.

She raised her head and looked at me with a confused, tired expression. "My vent? What do you—"

"Coffee!" Mitchell announced, pushing open the kitchen door suddenly and grinning. He set down a cup in front of Anika and she made a noise of approval before standing up and walking toward the fridge. When Mitchell finished setting down everyone's coffees, he sat down in the seat next to where Anika had been sitting and made eye contact with me. Something about the look in his eyes was unsettling; intimidating, almost.

What was that about?

# Chapter 24

*Foster*

Four days until the graduation party. I looked up at the ceiling of the room without much interest and contemplated this as I lay in bed. I would have to leave soon. So soon. Time needed to stop. It was only eight in the morning, and no one was likely to be awake yet, but every second longer that I spent in this room alone was a second I should've been with Anika. I closed my eyes. Rolling over yet again in an unsuccessful attempt to get comfortable enough to sleep for a little longer, I wished Anika was lying with me. I would sleep so easily with her in my arms.

I heard quiet talking outside of my room and stood up. I approached the door slowly and opened it.

Brady was standing with Anika, and she was looking down.

"Look Brady... I'm glad you're here, I really am, I just..." She kept looking at the ground.

"Is it Foster?"

"What?"

"Is he the reason you can't be happy that I'm here?"

Mitchell strode into the hallway, interrupting them. "Anika, your boxing class starts soon. Do you still want a ride or no?"

"Um... yeah, sure."

"Would you mind if I tagged along?" I asked, keeping my eyes locked on Anika.

"Oh, um, good morning," she said awkwardly. "You been awake very long?"

"No. Mitchell's voice woke me up."

He half glared at me but kept a relatively happy face for Anika. "I don't have much room in my car."

"I can help you make room."

Mitchell hesitated, trying to figure out how to get around letting me go with her.

"Sure, you can come," Anika piped up. "You just need to get dressed first."

"Of course."

Mitchell and I exchanged warning glances, and I didn't even notice Brady staring at me until I ducked back into my room.

***

Anika panted heavily as she finished her pyramids of ten on the kicking bag. She was strong, but she needed to work a little more on her stamina.

"Alright, everyone partner up for sparring!" the instructor announced.

I looked at Anika with a tilt to my head. "Be my partner?"

She laughed. "Yeah, right. I'm not sparring someone who could bench press me. Nice try, though. Besides, we switch partners every five minutes, so we'll be paired up eventually. I spar with Glen first, normally." Anika pointed to a small brunet guy who was grinning at her.

Irritated, I narrowed my eyes at the guy. Alright. I'd remember him.

I got paired with six people before I got to Glen. The second the instructor announced that we could begin, I slammed my instep into his ribs, sending him stumbling to the side. He scrambled to his feet and managed to get a kick to my shoulder, but I kicked him in the side again more forcefully in an attempt to get him to stay down. Finally, I did a turning kick into his side one more time and he didn't try to stand up; rather he sat on the ground, panting and looking up at me in mild surprise.

"Switch!"

I looked at Anika as she approached me and got a warm feeling in my body. My turn.

She raised an eyebrow at me and took her mouth piece out for a moment. "Are we going full out or are you gonna throw the match?"

"Would you like me to throw the match?"

"Hell no. I want to beat you fair and square." She grinned, slipping the mouthpiece in again, and getting her hands into position.

"Start!"

Anika and I started walking in circles, watching each other. I saw her arms twitch a little as she looked at where she wanted to punch, but I would immediately maneuver so that that area was protected. There was no chance in Hell of me hitting her, but I wouldn't just let her win, either. Her foot flashed out and slammed against my side, and I winced a little bit. She was strong. But, knowing her stamina, she'd run out of fuel after seven matches.

We continued circling each other for a little longer before she attacked again.

Her instep slapped against my arm and I grabbed it, twisting it over and pushing her away from me. She didn't fall—I'd made sure I didn't push hard enough for that—but she stumbled far enough that she hesitated before trying to kick me again.

After a while, she decided to try a punch. I caught her wrist, grabbing her other one as well, and hooked my leg behind one of hers, taking us both to the ground. I'd made sure to make most of my weight land on my forearms and elbows, which I'd put behind her back and head so she didn't hit the ground too hard. She panted hard and looked up at me.

Our faces were inches apart, and I had her pinned.

I grinned.

She rolled her eyes, still panting. "Shut up, I knew you'd win." Anika looked at me thoughtfully then leaned in her face a little.

I felt heat tinge my face as her lips almost brushed mine, then she shoved me to the side and pinned my arms and legs, grinning victoriously.

"Ha!" she declared, grinning, "I win!"

I rolled my eyes at her, smiling. I could break free any time I felt like it, but Anika pinning me down was not necessarily something I wanted to get out of. Lifting my head up, I hovered my lips just millimeters from her ear. "Good match," I murmured huskily. When I pulled back, she was bright red and I laughed. "You're cute when you blush."

"I'm not blushing," she protested, her voice shaking.

"Do I make you nervous?" I wondered aloud at the shaky tone.

"Shut up, Foster." She pushed off of me, stood up, then offered me her hand. I took it and stood up, looking down at her affectionately. "Good match," she said finally. "I'm not forgetting the fact that I won, either; I'm gonna hold that over your head forever, probably. So be prepared for a lifetime of 'remember that time I beat you?' coming your way."

I chuckled. "I wouldn't mind that." A lifetime of her saying that was a lifetime of being close enough to her for her to say it.

She rolled her eyes and punched me in the arm gently.

I smiled again.

"Class is over. I hope you all have a good day! Anika, you looked amazing today," the instructor yelled.

"Does he ever not yell? I'm contemplating cutting out his tongue," I muttered irritably.

"Do you ever not say something creepy?" she muttered, rolling her eyes.

I smirked. "Once in a while, maybe."

"Weirdo."

Mitchell honked his horn at us impatiently once we got through the doors and I looked at him thoughtfully, then at Anika.

"Anika, you said that Mitchell taught you to play chess, correct?"

"Yeah, for basically the past few years, why?"

I remembered her telling me that she still lost to him on purpose because she didn't want him to stop being her friend, and it brought a small smile to my lips. "I was thinking that the three of us could play against each other and we'd see how it plays out."

"Foster, did you just make a pun?"

"What?"

"Nothing, never mind."

Mitchell rolled down his window. "Um, guys? I still exist, here. Do you want to walk or something?"

Pressing my lips to turn upward, I smirked slightly at him. "Actually, Mitchell, we were discussing chess matters. I've heard you're rather decent at it, and I'd like for the three of us to play against one another." Of course, I had an alternative motive for wanting to play against him, but it wasn't like he could tell the difference, so what would be the point of bringing it up?

His eyes narrowed slightly with annoyance. "Normally, that's something that only Anika and I do together."

"If you think I'll beat you, then that's your choice, Mitchell."

"Fine."

Anika looked at him, then me, and I noticed her eyes widen innocently before she turned them on Mitchell. "Please, Mitchell? Come on, it'll be fun. He'll only play with us once then I'll play against you as long as you want me to when college rolls around."

He was clearly battling with himself over the options I'd presented him with, his head tilting slightly. "Anika…"

"Just one match!" she insisted.

A sharp sigh escaped his lips. "Fine, Anika, I'll play chess with both of you."

She nodded contently and looked up at me. "You just have to know how to bargain with him. He's a total pushover."

I'd like to push him over the edge of a cliff, if that counts.

# Chapter 25

I looked at the board in consideration, letting my head tilt to the side as I peered at it. If I moved my knight the way I wanted to, he would take it with his bishop, and I would take that with my rook, which would mean all he needed to do was sacrifice the queen and he'd have me in check in no more than two more moves after that point. My eyes flickered up to his face, where he met my gaze with his own, his eyes giving nothing away.

Tapping my knight on the top gently, I considered my options more thoroughly. His strategy was brilliant. The only way he'd even have a chance of losing was if he didn't give me his queen, and even then, it wasn't certain that I would be able to win from that point on. Finally, I gave in and moved my knight. After Mitchell then took it with his bishop, I took Mitchell's bishop with my rook, which proved to follow exactly in line with what I imagined.

Now all he needed to do was sacrifice his queen.

Mitchell caught his lip between his teeth for a minute, looking at the board in consideration, his eyes narrowed with concentration. His thumb tapped on the table for about fifteen seconds before he finally moved his bishop.

He wasn't going to give up the queen?

I raised an eyebrow slightly, moving my rook. "Check."

Mitchell chuckled briefly and blocked me with his pawn. If I took the pawn, I would get the piece taken by his king. For now, he was untouchable, but if I could manage to get my pawn there…

Charlie peeked her head over the table, slowly extending her hand toward the board.

"No, love," I murmured to her quietly, moving her hand away.

Charlie looked at me with bright blue orbs of curiosity, tilting her head and slowly inching her hand toward the board again. "I'm gonna play," she announced.

I laughed slightly. "I'll play a game with you in a minute, okay Charlie? Right now I'm playing with Mitchell."

She looked at the board which was hanging about an inch off of the table. "Fix!" Charlie smacked the edge of the board, probably trying to put it back on the table properly, but ended up sending it off the other side of the table.

Mitchell glared at her. "What was that, Charlie?" he snapped.

Her eyes widened. "I wanna help!"

"Well, you pushed the board off the edge."

"I-I didn't—"

"Don't do that again." He sighed sharply and got up. "I'm going to look for Anika so she can come get her sister out of the way." With that, he left the dining room.

Charlie's lip trembled and her eyes filled with tears, causing me to send an acidic glare Mitchell's way. I lowered myself from the chair to the floor so I could sit and be at eye level with her. She whimpered a little bit, sniffling and clumsily wiping her face, clearing it of tears that hadn't fallen yet.

"You're alright, Charlie."

She shook her head stubbornly, crossing her arms, her brown hair falling into her eyes. Her small body shook from having been scolded.

"Hey, Charlie, can I play chess against you?" I asked suddenly.

"No," she grumbled.

"Please? I really want to. Mitchell isn't as pretty as you. It would be more fun to play against a princess than a peasant."

The tears were gone soon after and she giggled loudly.

Offering her my hand, I feigned an inability to stand up. "Oh no, I think I need a strong girl to help me stand up. I'm really old. Do you know any super strong girls around here?"

"Anika!" she said immediately.

I chuckled. "Anyone a little closer?"

"…Mitchell," she decided.

The volume of my laughter startled her, but she laughed along soon enough, and smiled at me.

"Just kidding!" she chirped, "I'm really strong too!"

"I bet you are. You wanna help me up?"

Charlie nodded eagerly and grabbed my thumb and pinkie, using her entire weight and leaning back with effort to pull me up. I got to my feet, acting like she was pulling me up, and looked down at her. "Thank you. Now, do you want to play chess with me?"

She nodded again and scrambled into the chair opposite me.

I vaguely noticed Anika's presence as I explained to Charlie what the different pieces meant. After ignoring my crash course, Charlie insisted we play her way, which was a mixture of games.

"I have three horses. Black, white, black. I win."

"Is that how it works in Charlie Chess?"

"Mhmm," she hummed.

"Then do I win too, since the pattern on mine is black pawn, white pawn, black pawn?"

"Nope."

"Why?"

"'Cause those pieces are ugly."

"Makes sense."

Anika lowered herself to the floor in the doorway and raised a finger to her lips to warn me as she crawled toward Charlie's chair.

I waited until she was close, then widened my eyes. "Charlie! Oh no!"

She looked at me in confusion until Anika pulled the girl off the chair, causing her to squeal loudly. Anika grinned and tossed Charlie in the air slightly, then caught her again and brought her down to rest on top of her. "Did you have fun playing with Foster?"

"Mhmm."

"I think he's gonna try to take you home with him at this rate," she laughed.

142

Charlie looked up at me with wide eyes and started bouncing a lot, causing Anika to groan. "Will you really?"

This earned some laughter from me, but I picked her up so she wouldn't hurt her with the bouncing and set her on my lap. "You wouldn't want to live with me. It's dark there. Monsters live under my bed and in my closet."

"So? Maybe they're nice monsters."

"They aren't."

"They could be if you were nice to them too."

The logic of children is the purest in the world. She reminded me of Anika.

"Or you could beat them up," she added thoughtfully.

Yep, definitely reminded me of Anika.

Anika looked at us and smiled affectionately. "Hey, you two. I still exist."

"I'm very aware of your existence, Anika," I informed.

"You talk funny," Charlie commented.

"Yeah?"

"Yeah."

She swung her legs for a couple seconds before jumping off. "Imma get ice cream!" she said, toddling off in the direction of the kitchen.

Anika and I sat in silence for a few moments before she laughed. "I kind of don't want to move, honestly. The floor is comfortable."

Sliding myself from the chair again, I lay beside her and propped myself up on my elbow so that I could look at her. She smiled, shaking her head, and closed her eyes. "I missed you, Anika," I murmured to her quietly. She didn't reply and I reached out, touching her cheek gently. Still her eyes stayed closed. "Are you going to say something or should I keep staring at you?"

"I feel like you'd stare at me either way, so I'd rather pretend I don't know you're doing it."

"Fair enough," I chuckled.

"I missed you too."

Leaning in, I pressed my lips to her forehead gently.

"What the hell?"

Anika and I both jumped at Mitchell's yell, and I stood immediately, rushing to find where he was. He was in the living room, looking at Brady with widened eyes.

"You can't just bring a gun here, Brady, it's not a puppy!"

Brady snorted. "It's a gun. An inanimate object which doesn't hurt anyone unless someone uses it to hurt someone." Sure enough, in his hands were a loaded clip, a black handgun, and a receipt.

Mitchell opened his mouth to talk again but stopped himself before he could, then turned to look at Anika and me. "Anika, tell him he can't have a gun. That's insane."

"If I may," I interjected, "I don't think she can tell him not to own it, seeing that he bought it. Brady, may I ask you why you felt the urge to bring a gun into Anika's home?"

Completely ignoring my attempt to give him the opportunity to tell Anika about what he'd decided when she left, he shrugged. "I don't know. I saw it and wanted it and had money, so I figured I'd get it, you know?" His eyes skimmed over me, the intention of his look clear in his eyes; he wasn't ready for Anika to know yet. But what was the point in waiting?

"Ah, Brady? Guns kill people."

"Okay. Let's see." Brady pushed a clip into the gun and set it on the table, too close to Mitchell for my liking. He took a step back and gestured rather dramatically. "Go on, kill someone, gun." As we sat in silence, I could almost feel Anika's irritation growing beside me. "Go on, boy, do it," Brady encouraged sarcastically.

Mitchell raised his hand, causing me to stiffen, and he rubbed his temple. "You people give me headaches."

# Chapter 26

*Anika*

I looked at Foster, who appeared to be sleeping on the couch, then over at Brady; his eyes were set intensely on the screen, and I smirked slightly as he watched the children's movie. For someone who made a very adult-like move earlier today, he was a complete kid. Charlie had picked the cartoon movie out, and she was now asleep next to Foster, curled up against his side, her head on his shoulder and chest with her arm and leg across his body. It made me feel warm to see them getting along so well.

When I'd invited Foster, it had been because I missed the idea of him. He was completely harmless, kind of. Foster wasn't materialistic, or impatient, and even though he had one hell of a temper, he had never said anything to hurt me before. His strength was visible, both physically and mentally, and I always felt really secure around him, like nothing could happen while he was there. Then again, nothing probably could, now that I thought about it.

Charlie had taken to him immediately, and asked me if she could marry him, which made me smile. Now, looking at him with my little sister, asleep on the couch, I was pretty sure I'd missed a lot more than just the idea of him. I'd missed *him*.

Brady, on the other hand…

By the time I had left, I had figured out that things weren't going well between us. We had the passion, but what did I really know about him? Foster asked questions about me, letting me spend hours of his time just talking, because he was interested in learning about me. Brady never asked me anything. He just called me pretty and told me I mattered to him. I was pretty sure that was called infatuation.

*Love* on the other hand... Love was slow. It wasn't the spark of passion that infatuation was. It was something gentle and safe that couldn't be broken. I could love Foster. I was certain of it. Who wouldn't love someone like that? Someone so devoted to your every action?

Foster's eyelids lifted and he looked at me, smiling slightly.

He had the kind of smile that could make someone contact-high. It wasn't often that he did it, but when he did... Oh, man. Sometimes the pure art of his expressions was astounding to me. He was just so pleasant when he wasn't being kind of insane. Maybe he just didn't know how to show it. Didn't wolves kill things they loved sometimes?

The thought chilled my blood a little, but I knew Foster. He would never lay a finger on me in a harmful way. I wasn't sure how I knew that, but I did.

My fingers found their way to the necklace around my neck, and I slowly traced the penguin design, closing my eyes once Foster had closed his as well. I continued tracing the penguin for a while, then eventually traced his name with my finger, and I fell asleep with a smile on my face. Love was really weird.

***

*Foster*

I opened my eyes, looking down at the little girl on top of me. Her head had fallen slightly to face the couch, and I gently used my free hand to move her back onto my shoulder again. Her hair was messy and wild from sleep, and I smoothed my hand over it to tame it as gently as I could.

Maybe one day, I would have this again; a little girl with brown hair and blue eyes curled up on top of me, with Anika beside me. If it was what Anika wanted in her future, I would make it happen for her. Even if she didn't want children, that was something I could

146

accept as well. All I could accomplish by having a child would be passing along something to a small human; a beautiful, clean slate that knew nothing about the world.

Briefly, the image of a little boy with big blue eyes and black hair flashed through my mind, causing a smile to light my lips gingerly.

There was some kind of myth among people that girls were the only ones that dreamed about weddings and what their children would look like and their future. Why do people think men are so different? I wanted a life with Anika as much as any girl could dream of her own prince. Every morning that I got to wake up and see her was like Christmas to me. She was the greatest gift I'd ever gotten in my life, after all.

I wasn't obsessive over her, I was thankful. She gave me my life; my confidence. She gave me a will and a reason. Anika gave me everything I wanted, simply by existing.

My gaze drifted to Brady. He'd stayed awake through the movie and was now scrolling aimlessly through the list of movies on the screen. He would look at Anika every now and then, his focus only ever on her briefly. Then again, that was probably perfectly representative of his "love" of her.

Mitchell walked in, a grim look on his face, and I sat up slowly when I saw his demeanor. Something had happened.

"What is it?" I asked immediately.

He glared at me slightly. "Wake Anika up."

"Why?"

"Wake her up."

I waited, ignoring his demand, and he finally leaned over, touching her shoulder gently.

Anika blinked open her eyes, yawning, and stretched a little bit, grumbling about being woken up. Her hair fell across her face messily and her eyes were still hazy from the veil of sleep. "What, Mitchell?" she mumbled at him as she stretched her back.

"Don't panic, but your dad just called, and he's in the hospital."

"What?" Anika half yelled, her eyes wide and her pupils dilated with fear. Well, she was definitely awake now. Uneasiness flooded my body hearing the news.

147

Mitchell put his hands on her shoulders. "Anika, it's okay. He got dizzy working on one of the cars and passed out. He hit his head a little, but he'll be fine. They just need to do a little bit of testing and check out the rest of his system to make sure he's really okay."

"We need to go." She whirled this way and that, looking around. "Where are my keys?"

Brady had uncertainty plastered on his face.

We both knew that Jensen was a little more ill than he'd been letting on. How severe, though, was yet to be determined. I prayed that the tests they were going to perform on him would go smoothly. I didn't like the idea of Anika seeing him buried either.

The loud clatter of metal against metal sounded —Anika had obviously found her keys—and I stood, moving Charlie so that she was seated on my forearm, her head over my shoulder and my other arm on her back.

"I'll drive," Mitchell offered.

She looked at him thankfully and nodded, looking at me. "Foster, I have to go. I'll see you when I get home, okay? Just stay here and… don't hurt Brady, I guess." Anika disappeared through the door quickly.

Mitchell looked at me. "Sorry I can't take you with me," he lied through a smile.

"Mitchell!" Anika yelled from outside.

He chuckled and walked out, following her.

Then it was just Brady and me.

# Chapter 27

As Brady scrolled through the movies on the screen, I looked at him in consideration. "Do you intend to tell Anika that you're here because you want to see her before going into the military?"

He stopped moving, but didn't say anything.

"She has a right to know, Brady."

"I'm an adult. I'll do what I want with my life, got it?" His tone was hard, and he turned his steely eyes on me. "You don't say one word to her about that. Understand me? I'll tell her when I leave." Brady turned to the screen again, clearly annoyed. "Besides, what would she care? She doesn't love me the way I love her."

"You don't love her at all, Brady."

"Don't you dare tell me what I do and don't feel, creep. You don't know anything about me."

"Brief glimpses into the concept of loving someone paired with sexual attraction is just infatuation, Brady. You're in pain over her because you created some fake relationship with her in your head and let yourself get emotionally invested in it. If you let go of the relationship in your mind, you'll stop being in pain." I let a sympathetic smile slide onto my lips, trying to offer compassion of sorts. "It's understandable. But I've seen the way you look at her. It's not with love. It's with jealousy or lust."

"Shut up, Foster."

"I'm trying to help you."

"You're *trying* to piss me off, and it's working," he growled.

"Brady, how much time have you been spending with Sierra as of late?"

149

When I suddenly mentioned the small blonde, I felt his entire vibe change. Instead of anger, he was hesitant and confused. "Anika has been blowing me off for most of the time I've been here. So yeah, I've been spending time with Sierra. What's your point?"

"Has it occurred to you that she may be attracted to you?"

Sighing, Brady tossed the controller to the end of the couch. "Sierra went to a hotel the second she found out Anika was a room short. She's barely seen her, and Sierra is the entire reason I was able to come, so yes, I do spend time with her. That doesn't mean that we're attracted to each other. I mean, yeah, she's cute and all, but come on. She's so loud and... yappy. Like a small dog or something. I'd never be into someone like her, man. I'm after Anika."

"Thou doth protest too much."

"Could you shut up and be normal for a few minutes? I'm not taking relationship advice from someone who stalks the person they're interested in."

"The time without her helped me to contemplate myself and the way I handle things. I'm not who I was, Brady, and I don't believe you are, either." He looked at me in consideration and I slowly started toward my next statement. "With that being said, I've got a favor to ask you."

"Why should I do anything for you?"

"Because Anika is involved."

There was silence for a moment. "I'm listening."

"Mitchell. He changed as well." I sat forward and rested my elbows on my knees. "We aren't the only ones who were turned in a one-eighty by Anika's leaving. By leaving, Anika essentially cast him into a year of solitude since he has no other friends. He changed for the worse. There's something in his eyes that makes me even more wary than I was, and I don't know if he's safe or how much more it would take to push him over the edge. So I need you to stay until the party is over, and I'll do my best to take it from there."

His eyebrows pulled upwards and he sat back slightly. "You picked up on that too?"

"Yes."

"I always knew the guy was a little weird. Someone said that he had to come to our middle school because he got his family practically kicked out of the neighborhood for… doing something, but I figured someone like that would appear a lot more… off than he does." His tone was doubtful and his eyebrows had pushed together now as he thought more in depth about who Mitchell was and how he acted.

"Actors do the same thing every day," I said seriously. "That's what he does. I can see it in his twitching, in his voice, and in the way he moves that he forces himself to appear to be who he is so that he can stay with Anika. Are you going to stay or not?"

"I'll stay."

"I'm holding you to that."

"Go ahead." He shrugged, then peered at me from the corner of his eye. "You think Sierra is interested in me?"

I fought off my smile and nodded.

Brady nodded slightly and I left him to think so that I could look around Mitchell's room while he was gone.

The door creaked open quietly in protest to my pushing, and I looked around slowly. It was neat and clean, but wires from chargers, headphones, and computer systems were set up here and there. Honestly, I wouldn't have been surprised if he had pictures of her plastered everywhere on his walls with hearts drawn in blood around them, but there was no sign of anything like that yet.

There wasn't time for me to go through all of this. Any minute, one of them could come back; maybe Anika had forgotten something here. Or perhaps Mitchell had cameras set up in his room. There was no telling.

I tilted my head in consideration then walked back out to where Brady was. "You've rented a car, right?"

"Uh, yeah. Why?"

"I'd like to go see Anika and her father now."

# Chapter 28

*Brady*

I glanced at Foster from the corner of my eye as we drove. His eyes were set on the window, and I took the time to think. I'd had a lot of time to think since I'd arrived.

Anika had busied herself mostly with Foster and Mitchell, even after I'd gotten there. So, because of that, I'd been going out and doing things with Sierra. Yes, she was annoying, but at the same time, she'd been the only person I really stuck with after Anika left. Foster and I hadn't interacted much, Mitchell had dropped off the map, and it was just her.

That didn't mean I was attracted to her, though. Honestly, I wasn't sure what I felt for anyone at this point anymore. My hatred of Foster became jealousy then just mild distaste. My attitude toward Mitchell had turned into just a suspicious uncomfortable feeling. And Anika...

She would probably hate me for telling her I was going into the army soon. She'd tell me it wasn't safe, and that she didn't want me getting hurt. It wasn't her call, though.

I'd never put thought into what I'd do with my future. I was just a kid after all. The concept of my future barely ever came into real light, no matter how many times my mom or teachers brought it up. College wasn't going to happen for me, but I wasn't going to flip burgers for a living either. There was no direction that I was pointed in. So why not the army? I'd be taking care of my country. My mother was proud of my choice, even though she was terrified. It wasn't like I had much of a life here, anyway.

"Brady!"

I slammed on the brakes hard when I realized I was at a stop sign, only to have someone honk at me. Driving isn't something I should be doing when I'm not focused.

As I pulled up into the parking lot of the hospital, I looked at Foster again from the corner of my eye.

He was really into Anika. I knew that much. Even though I still didn't like him all that much, I could acknowledge that he'd give Anika a life. His father was loaded. Even if he weren't, though, I felt like Foster would have still loved her. What had made me love her in the first place? The fact that I couldn't have her? I shook my head to clear that thought away, convincing myself that I wasn't that shallow.

Truth was, though, that even while I was moping around over Anika for the past few months... I wasn't sure how much of that was really about missing her. *Ugh, this is why I don't think. It sucks.*

Foster and I approached the room, and even if I hadn't known Anika's voice, I could have still figured out who was who by the words being exchanged.

"No, you're going to sit there and let them treat you instead of being a stubborn ass about everything."

"Anika," Jensen started.

"No."

"Can you just—"

"Nope."

How Anika of her.

I knocked on the doorframe gently to get their attention.

Anika had been standing in front of Jensen, who looked like he was trying to stand up, with her arms crossed. When her eyes caught me, the annoyance faded slightly, and she sighed. "Oh, hey you two. Did you see Sierra on the way in? I called her."

"I didn't see anyone," Foster informed her.

Mitchell was sitting on the bed beside her father, his arm around Jensen's shoulders as he sat up. He looked at me with slightly narrowed eyes and a subtle tilt to his head that I didn't like.

"I was worried about your dad," I piped up.

A bandage was pressed to his forehead with blood smeared on it, causing me to grimace slightly.

"What, you don't like blood?" Mitchell asked. "I can only imagine how you'll do in your future career."

I stiffened and shot my gaze to Foster, but he didn't give anything away. The only people who knew were me, Sierra, my mother, and Foster because he was somehow a freaky omniscient being or something. "The point is, we're both here now, okay? How's…" My voice trailed off as I noticed a brace on Anika's foot. "What's that about?"

Her hand went to the back of her neck as she moved her eyes to the ground. "Nothing," she grumbled.

"Anika got into a fight with a nurse who said she couldn't come back here to see me," Jensen sighed tiredly. "She tripped and twisted her ankle pretty bad. She's gonna be in a boot for a week or so, probably."

"You fought a nurse?" I asked her in surprise.

Anika glared at me a little. "No, a nurse fought *me*."

"…Right."

Foster knelt in front of her on one knee and inspected the boot with interest. He looked up at her as he twisted the boot very carefully. "Does this hurt?"

"No."

He nodded and twisted it in the other direction, only slightly, and she inhaled sharply.

"Could you not do that?" Mitchell muttered.

"I'm just testing something."

"You're 'testing' my patience."

"I'd be disappointed with my result."

"Enough," Anika snapped suddenly. "Look, my dad has to stay here for a few days, so can we all just go for now? We have to look after Charlie and my mom's gonna come look after Dad while he's here. He's gonna be back sometime after my party."

I nodded to her. "I'm glad he's okay."

A light, quick tapping at the door sounded and Sierra ran into the room, skidding to a halt suddenly. "Is Jensen okay? What's wrong with Anika's leg? Does her mom know? Who's watching Charlie? Oh God, I think I'm going to be sick."

"Calm down," I sighed.

Sierra threw her arms around me suddenly and my body stiffened in surprise, but I relaxed a moment later. "Uh, question. Why are you hugging me exactly?"

"Because I need to hug someone and two of the five people I can hug are injured, and the other one is Foster."

"Sierra," Anika snapped lightly.

A deep chuckle told me he wasn't offended and Anika raised an eyebrow at me slightly from over Sierra's head. I shook my head, telling her I had no idea, and she shrugged, turning her attention back to Foster. Slight disappointment tinged my mood, and Sierra's grip on me tightened. I let my hands go to her back, and I rubbed gently in circles. "Everyone's alive, Sierra," I muttered quietly. "That's what matters."

"For now," Mitchell pointed out. "Everyone dies."

"Ah, Mitchell? Not the time," Anika half growled.

"Right. My bad."

She looked up at me. "Can you drive me home, Brady?"

"Actually, I was gonna ask him that," Sierra cut in abruptly. "I kind of took a taxi here 'cause I was in a panic."

"I'll take you home," Mitchell offered.

"Where's Foster going, then?"

"I can find myself a ride," he assured me.

Anika hesitated, catching her lip in her teeth. As I looked at her eyes, then down at Sierra, I couldn't help but think about how funny it was the way life worked.

# Chapter 29

*Foster*

There was a knock on my door. "Foster?" Anika's hushed whisper came.

"Mm?" I muttered back drowsily from my state between sleep and consciousness.

"Do you mind if I sleep in here?"

I sat up, no longer half asleep. She had my full attention. "I don't mind." Through the darkness, I could barely make out her appearance. She was in shorts and a t-shirt, and her hair was messy from sleep, but other than that I couldn't make out any details.

Pressure forced the bed down slowly next to me, and I lifted up the blanket I was under to cover her. She silently curled against me, and I lay on my side, just watching her. Leaning over, I gently pressed my lips to her forehead, and lay on my back again.

"Is that all you're going to try on me?" she asked suddenly.

Heat tinged my face in the darkness despite the amused smirk on my lips. "Would you have let me try anything else?"

"Nope."

This earned a short laugh from me, and I smiled, shaking my head. That was Anika, alright.

She sighed and rolled onto her side, facing me now, and rested her head on my shoulder. Her hand rested on my torso, and I looked for a reaction from her; I wasn't wearing a shirt. She didn't say anything about it, so I relaxed, beyond content to even feel her beside me.

"Why did you invite me here, Anika?"

Her shoulder shifted against me in a shrug, and I shook my head.

"Come on. That isn't an answer. Why'd you let me come here?"

"Do you wish I hadn't?"

"I was going to come eventually."

She sighed quietly. "I missed you. You know that." Her ankle brace scratched against my leg and I shifted my foot away, moving it to the other side of the bed.

"And why didn't you invite Brady?"

She sat up slowly, looking down at me for a moment before looking away. "Brady and I are going to lead very different lives. He's who he is, and I'm who I am. Sometimes people just don't work well together, you know?"

I nodded. "And... we *do* work well together?"

"Better than me and Brady."

"Alright." I laid my head back down again and looked up at the dark ceiling.

Though she hadn't said it, I was almost certain she'd just chosen me.

\*\*\*

*Mitchell*

I stirred, the light from the window bothering my eyes. There were no sounds, just the silence of morning. Which, I guess, was normal for Anika's house, without her father awake to force her to get out of bed.

Picking up a picture of Anika I'd had printed, I hummed quietly and pinned it next to the other ones on the board in my suitcase. I had a picture of her from almost every year of her life that I'd known her. She was just so beautiful to look at.

As I wandered down the hall, I tapped on her door lightly. "C'mon, Anika, you gotta wake up this year."

157

Nothing.

"Anika," I repeated softly, pushing on her door. It gave way, swinging open lazily and I peered into the sunlight-flooded room. Her blankets were bunched and spread; she'd always been an aggressive sleeper. One thing was missing from this picture, though.

Her.

Curious, I walked from her room to the kitchen, trailing my fingers over the table slowly. She wasn't in there either. I opened the fridge and several cupboards, but none of her dishes seemed moved, so she hadn't eaten yet today, which was very unlike her.

"Come on, Anika," I hummed lightly, inspecting the knife I'd pulled from a drawer. "Where are you?"

Just as I expected, though, the silence didn't reveal her location. A pain in my temple hit and I rubbed it slowly, closing my eyes as the world turned fuzzier and watching the colors distort slightly. Soon enough, though, it was gone. It always went away. I could see the world more easily when it was there, though. I could see it how it was.

Wandering farther still, I saw Brady's gun in its case on the counter beside the microwave. What an irresponsible thing to do.

Holding the cold metal, I tilted my head. I'd always wanted to shoot a gun. I'd never had the opportunity before, though, nor the proper target. I was certain I would be a good hunter if I tried it, however. Hunting would be quite a fascinating experience; the adrenaline, the hunt, the actual kill.

Fascinating.

I decided it was time to check on Foster. He was one irritating bug, that one. As I walked to his room, I chuckled at my stupidity. "Oops," I laughed, setting the knife on the ground. I'd forgotten to put it down, and Foster would probably try to hurt me if he thought I was threatening him. Foster was one of many I would never be able to remove by myself just with brute force. He was much too large for that. However, I was confident I could outsmart him. He'd be gone soon enough, though, and it would be over.

"Foster?" I chirped, pushing his door open.

What was inside, however, made me freeze.

That's where Anika was.

Her head was on his bare chest, only her bare legs exposed from under the blanket she'd pulled over her shoulder. Was she... naked?

My heart beat wildly, though fury was not a word I could place to the sensation. It felt like something was breaking. Perhaps my bond with her.

Either way, I just stood, staring.

He'd ruined her.

I was so patient. *So* patient, waiting for so long for her to be mine. And yet she'd given herself to someone else. Someone like him. He wasn't me. It should have been me.

Very slowly, I slid backward from the room, and went to sit in the living room.

I wanted nothing more than to grab the nearest thing and throw it, but I didn't want to wake them. All I wanted was time to process what I'd just seen, and how I would handle it.

One thing was for sure: it was over.

It was all over, for all of them. All of *us*.

My eyes caught the gleam of the gun I'd moved from the kitchen to behind the television, out of sight. It was out of its case now, loaded, and merely hidden beside a television and a wall.

Curious, the ideas that swim through a jealous man's head.

Though my eyes burned, I knew what had to happen. This had to be the end for her as much as it was for me. I slid my hands to the back of my neck, placing my elbows on my knees and rocking slightly.

Maybe it didn't. Maybe.

After all, I did love her.

But she broke me. She had to be punished. All of them did. *She made the wrong choice*, my inner self whispered reasonably. *She has to suffer the consequences of her choice, just as any other person would. She's an adult now. Don't treat her like a child. Obviously she's been doing things that aren't exactly childlike.* A strange calmness came over my body as I sat up.

Perhaps calmness wasn't the word?

It was more like certainty. I was certain. They all had to go.

# Chapter 30

*Anika*

My arms were locked around Mitchell's waist as I hugged him, burying my face against his shoulder. "Thank you for telling me," I murmured quietly. "Someone needed to. I can't believe he didn't tell me himself."

"Are you angry with him?"

"I'm seething," I laughed briefly as my voice cracked.

"Alright." Mitchell's hand smoothed over my hair, his head tilted. "Don't go too hard on him."

"Are you kidding me? His ass is *out* of my house. Today."

His eyes widened in surprise. "Your party starts in like an hour. You're just gonna kick him out without giving him a reason?"

"Oh, I'll give him a reason," I growled. I sighed, hugging Mitchell again and looking into his eyes. "Are you okay?" I asked slowly, noticing that his eyes seemed a little more empty and glazed than usual.

"Hm? I'm fine." He offered me an artificial grin.

"Okay. Thank you for telling me. I really appreciate it." I finally stepped back from him. "You really are my best friend, Mitchell. I love you."

The smile stayed in place, but it didn't seem any more real to me than it had been before. "I love you too, Anika, trust me." His voice had lowered, and I felt slight chills on my body when he said it, like something wasn't right. But I didn't have time to think about it. I had bigger fish to fry, and *damn*, did I plan to fry him to a crisp.

"What is wrong with you?" I yelled the second I saw him.

Brady and Foster looked up in surprise, eyes widened in confusion.

I jabbed my finger at Brady. "You're joining the army."

Immediately the color fled from his face, and his eyes shot to Foster.

My body shook slightly as a moment of realization came over me. "You knew?" I asked Foster numbly.

"He asked me not to tell you," Foster murmured gently.

Brady stood up, walking toward me. "It wasn't his information to tell, Anika. Look, I was going to tell you before I left, I just figured you didn't need to know that yet. It would've hurt you."

"And this doesn't?" I half screeched, my voice shooting up an octave but trembling violently. It felt like part of me was being torn away, even though he and I weren't close anymore. He was someone I'd known for almost my entire life. "You're going to die," I whispered.

He shook his head slowly. "No, I'm not."

"You are!" I snapped, my eyes filling with tears. "You're literally going off somewhere to be shot and killed!"

"That's not what I'm doing, Anika."

"Then what are you doing?!"

"Living for me for once!" he yelled back, shaking. As I stood there, not speaking and instead just staring at him without understanding, he took a deep breath. "I waited for you Anika. I did. I'm so tired of waiting. I want to do something with my life, something good. I've never done anything good for anyone, and that makes me dread being who I am." He shook his head as if trying to will me into understanding. "I'm going to do this no matter what you say."

"I don't want you here," I whispered. "If you're going to die, I don't want to watch you go off to do it."

"You know," he laughed angrily, "I almost thought that you would want me to do something for myself. I *almost* believed that you would be happy that I found something I wanted to do." His eyes skimmed my face furiously for a moment before he turned sharply. "Whatever," he hissed as he walked. "I'm leaving."

"Good!"

"Fine!"

"*Fine!*"

The door to his room slammed hard enough to make the walls shake slightly, and I felt like falling to my knees and sobbing.

Mitchell's hand touched my shoulder gently, and he kissed the top of my head.

I tore away from him. "Don't."

"Two," I heard him murmur under his breath quietly.

"What?"

"Are you okay?"

I laughed dryly in response.

Foster stood up and looked down at me. "Anika—"

"Shut up."

His mouth closed reluctantly, and he nodded slowly.

I took a deep breath. "We have a party to get ready for. Guests will be here any second. There's a lot of people coming. So if you want to say anything, make it related to my party, and make it useful, because I am *going* to enjoy myself today, no matter what you say."

Foster nodded again.

"Okay." I took another shallow breath and the doorbell went. Brushing down my pants as though I was wiping away the anger, I plastered a smile on my face, though tears tore at me internally. "Let's have a party, then."

# Chapter 31

*Foster*

Anika laughed and hugged Sierra around the neck, pulling the small blonde close to her and grinning. I couldn't hear what she was saying from here, but it was probably just thanks for her gift.

I sipped from my punch slowly. It tasted like watered-down gummy bears, and I didn't like it, but I needed something to do. While Anika was surrounded by friends and family for the past few hours, I'd been trying to keep my eye on Mitchell. He'd come in on me sleeping next to Anika, and there was no telling what had happened to him and his fragile mind.

People had started leaving already, leaving only a few drunken family members scattered about.

Sierra hugged Anika again, then walked off. Well, skipped off.

I chuckled quietly as I watched them and approached Anika. "You having fun?"

Her eyes were tired, but happy. "Yeah."

"How does your ankle feel?"

"Like it's being cut off."

"That doesn't sound healthy."

"It's probably not, honestly."

I smirked slightly. "Then go sit down for a bit."

"Nah."

"You kicked Brady out?" Sierra's voice came, small and disbelieving.

164

Anika sighed and turned to the girl who I hadn't noticed approaching us. "No. He left. We had an argument over his stupid—"

"Over him joining the army?"

Though her mouth fell open slightly, Anika quickly closed it. "You knew too."

"Of course I knew, I'm his... friend," said Sierra. She fidgeted slightly and glowered at me. "Did Foster have anything to do with it? Is he why you made Brady leave? He only decided to join because he wants to do some good, Anika. It's not our choice."

"He had nothing to do with it," Anika sighed.

"Do you care if I leave early to go see him?" Sierra asked nervously.

"Of course not."

Sierra nodded and took off in a small jog toward the house, disappearing soon after, and Anika groaned quietly. "My ankle is killing me," she grumbled again.

"Sit down for a bit."

Anika looked past me and waved at someone a little. "Mitchell! Can you grab a few chairs and come over here?"

My stomach twisted uneasily. I didn't want him here. The sooner he left, the better.

He was upon us within a few seconds with a few fold-up chairs tucked under his arm. "Here we go," he chimed, setting them out. A smile was spread across his lips, and he was unsettlingly... neutral.

"So, college girl," Mitchell smiled, leaning back in his chair. "You excited? We're down to one."

"One?"

"It's just us and Foster," he reminded her cheerily. "Then when he leaves, it's off to college."

Anika laughed a little. "Oy, don't remind me. I don't need to feel older than I already do."

"Foster, would you go get a CD for me?" Mitchell requested in a civil tone, looking at me expectantly. "It's in my suitcase. And take your time, I have some things to say to Anika that I'd rather say

165

alone. It's her favorite CD," he added, urging me to go get it once he saw me hesitating.

"Please?" Anika asked eagerly.

I looked between them uncertainly. "Alright," I gave in eventually.

She smiled up at me. "Thanks, Foster."

"Of course."

***

Anika

I looked at Mitchell, smiling at him as Foster disappeared toward the house. "So, what CD is it?"

"A special one," he purred lightly. "Would you like to dance with me?"

"There's no music, you dork," I scoffed.

Mitchell raised his eyebrows. "I don't think that's what I asked."

After a moment of consideration, I nodded, standing up and looking at him. "Alright, fine. Only because you were such a huge help today, though." I sighed. "It's a good thing I love you. I can barely stand right now."

"Why? Your ankle?"

"Yeah. It sucks."

"You shouldn't have fought a nurse." Mitchell smiled, shaking his head. "Step on my feet."

I grinned. "I don't think there was doubt about me stepping on your feet. I'm not the most graceful of dancers." Still, I slipped off my one shoe and stood on his feet. His arms were around my waist, holding me securely as he swayed us slightly.

"You know, Anika, you've made more mistakes than just fighting a nurse."

My amusement was gone immediately. "Yeah. So what? Everyone has."

"Mistakes that are going to get you hurt."

"What doesn't kill you makes you stronger," I muttered.

"Interesting choice of phrase." Mitchell dipped me back, leaning me backward over his arm and looking down at me. Something scary was in his eyes. I'd never seen it before.

"L-let me up, okay? I'm done dancing."

"So am I. Because we're at zero now."

"What are you talking about? Mitchell, you're starting to freak me out. Let go." I squirmed, but only one of his hands left my waist.

"No." Something sharp touched my back and I flinched, pressing against him. A cold grimace of a smile hinted at his face. "I'm going to show you what it's like to be stabbed in the back like you did to me."

"Mitchell," I repeated shakily, squirming away from the blade and trembling in fear. "Stop it! Get off of me!"

"No!" His eyes lost their cool, a wild look overtaking them now. He was shaking, and his eyes pooled with furious tears. "You need to feel what it's like! What it was like for me!"

"I don't know what you're talking about! Stop it! Foster!" I shrieked.

"Mitchell," a deep voice snapped.

Immediately I was spun around, twisting my ankle in a way which caused me to scream. Mitchell was wielding a large knife.

And it was pointed directly at Foster.

# Chapter 32

*Foster*

I held out my hand toward Mitchell slowly as if putting my hand there would convince him not to do anything rash. "Mitchell," I tried carefully, "you're sick. We know you're sick, and we aren't mad, but I need you to put that knife down before you do something you'll regret, okay? We don't need to do it like this. Let go of Anika, and we'll talk about this."

His jaw clenched, his eyes full of tears. "Shut up!"

"Mitchell," I repeated more softly, "you don't want to hurt her, right? You love her."

"I can understand her loving someone else even while I love her," he snarled suddenly. "I can be patient while she kisses other people." Mitchell yanked the knife away from her and pointed it at me. "But she slept with *you*!" he yelled shakily. "You! I've been here for years, never not loving her, and you come in and just... just, take her!"

Anika was frozen in place, her eyes locked on me desperately as her lips shook and tears slipped down her cheeks.

"If you just calm down, we can talk about this."

"I don't want to talk anymore!"

"Okay, would you like to propose a fight, then?" I offered quietly.

He laughed sharply. "I'm not that stupid, Foster." His crazed eyes were still full of tears. "You know why I drugged her? You want to know why? I mean you clearly do, you asked me, right?" Mitchell exposed his teeth in a sickening grin and he shook his head slightly. "It's simple. If she got drugged while you were there, it would've

168

been your fault. She would've left you alone. You'd have been arrested. But you," he growled through his smile angrily, "you saw me. You ruined everything. You ruined my entire life. You ruined *her*!"

Anika's legs were shaking now from how stiffly she was standing in place. "Mitchell," she whimpered.

"No!" He tore his arm from the air and pressed the blade to her neck.

"I didn't sleep with him!" she cried, shaking.

"Don't lie to me!"

I took several steps forward instinctively, now just four feet from him. He swung the knife wildly toward me with wide eyes. Keeping my arms steady at my sides, I looked him in the eye. If I was going to help her at all, I needed to play into what he believed to be the truth. "I know not seeing her drove you a little more insane," I murmured. "I know me sleeping with her put you over the edge. But Mitchell, think. Think about how long you've been friends with her. How happy she makes people. You can hate me, and you can hate her, but do you hate the world enough to take her away from it?"

His jaw clenched and unclenched, and Mitchell squeezed his eyes closed hard for a moment, before opening them with a calm look that made fear and certainty form in the pit of my stomach. Once more, he let his smile come to his face, though his eyes were absolutely empty. "Yes." The veins in his arms bulged slightly as he prepared to move.

Anika slammed her elbow into him suddenly, into his chest, and he groaned loudly. Tears were running down her face as she threw her leg back hard, trying blindly to land a kick. "I'm sorry Mitchell!" she sobbed as she kicked out more, stumbling toward me the best she could with her brace on. I grabbed her as soon as I could reach her and yanked her behind me, launching myself onto Mitchell almost at the same time.

He let out an almost animalistic screech and squirmed on the ground as I used my bodyweight against him, pressing on his chest as hard as I could manage. Mitchell swung his arm, catching my arm with his knife, and I immediately turned my attention to trying to get the knife out of his hand. It would be hours until Anika's father was home, which meant I needed to get Mitchell down, and fast, because I wouldn't last a few hours.

Mitchell dug his fingers into the cut in my arm viciously, pushing past the skin, and pain seared my body so intensely that I couldn't move. He shoved me off of him and got on top of me. I could hear Anika screaming.

It was all happening so quickly: Mitchell pulling the knife above his head, ready to plunge it down into me, a man's voice...

And then a gunshot, followed by pain.

A scream tore its way from Mitchell's throat as he fell over to the side, grabbing his bleeding side desperately, and my hand flew to my shoulder where the bullet had nicked the top. I looked around for the knife, grabbing it and hurling it over the fence.

I fell onto the ground again, panting hard, and lay with my eyes closed. Stabbed *and* shot? What a Saturday.

Anika screamed my name repeatedly and I felt her body on top of mine as she searched for other places I was hurt. I shook my head, still panting.

"I'm okay," I huffed.

Her arms wove around me and she buried her face against me, shaking hard. I put my good hand on her back and looked behind her at the person who had shot Mitchell.

Brady had finally been of some use in my life.

\*\*\*

The paramedic pressed another bandage to my shoulder and I grimaced, then turned to look at Anika and Brady.

"Thank you, Brady," Anika said to him quietly.

Brady gave a slight grin. "I've always wanted to shoot Foster."

I smirked.

"Why did you come back, though?"

His hand went to the back of his neck, rubbing slightly. "I forgot my gun."

"Oh."

170

A silence settled, and I cleared my throat. Anika looked at me and offered a smile, and she brought Brady over to me. "I think you have something to say to Brady, Foster."

"Thanks for not hitting any vital organs."

"I aimed for your head," he dismissed with mock disappointment.

"You mean Mitchell's head?"

Brady grinned again. "Yeah, that."

I chuckled and shook my head. "You're a horrid shot."

Sierra approached, looking at all of us nervously. "Where's... Where's Mitchell?"

"Cop car."

She nodded slowly, then cast her gaze at Brady. "You're a lifesaver, you know that?" Sierra hesitated, then stood on the tips of her toes and pressed her lips to Brady's cheek, turning bright red.

I chuckled, giving Brady a knowing look as he let his arm fall around her waist.

Anika smiled at them slightly, giving a small nod, and laid her head against my shoulder. Then, the four of us just stood there in the flashing red and blue lights.

# Chapter 33

Anika licked the spoon in her hand slowly, eyeing me. "And how exactly did you get admitted to my college last second?"

"The things money will buy," I hummed innocently.

She scowled at me half-heartedly. "Look. I said I'd date you, but that doesn't mean you can go around throwing money around everywhere, got it? It's stupid."

I shrugged and took a bite of her ice cream.

She made a quiet yelping noise. "Hey!"

"Could you two not share food in front of me?" Jensen groaned. "It's enough that I let you stay here for college, I don't need to see you doing... couple stuff." He gestured, and I grinned, leaning away from Anika obediently.

"Yes, sir."

She smiled warmly at me. "Ha. I win. Get your own next time."

"I already did." Raising an eyebrow, I chuckled and shook my head, "You moved half of it to your bowl, remember?"

"Details," she dismissed.

"Right."

Jensen took a swig from his drink, and I could see him smiling from behind the mug as he watched us. We'd be starting our classes in a few months, but it didn't matter to me when we did. I was ready for it. For the next chapter of my life, with a beautiful love interest at my side, and no messy love triangle to screw with it.

The birds sang louder now, and everything smelled better; even Jensen's burnt coffee.

I'd always believed that once they locked eyes, people destined for each other would never truly look away again. My eyes had been set on Anika since the day we met, even when she wasn't there anymore. I guess I saw with my heart. Maybe that's why I'd been able to see through Mitchell's ruse.

He wasn't evil. He was just sick. He was a sick, sick boy who no one had helped over time. He'd tried so hard to hold on, I knew that. But sometimes, you just can't anymore. At least, he couldn't. And because of that, I couldn't fully hate him for what he did, and I knew Anika didn't either.

I looked at Anika now. It'd been a month since everything went down with Mitchell. Sierra was back home, and Brady... I wasn't sure where he was at the moment.

Knowing my luck though, he'd show up again soon enough.

I'd thrown out my cameras in the recent weeks; there was no need for them anymore. She was safe now, and I was going to spend—hopefully—the rest of my life keeping her that way. Sure, our love story had started out pretty screwy, but she'd changed me.

Love was weird. But I didn't want to understand it. It was poetically chaotic, and beautifully messy.

Our lives together started with Mitchell and Sierra, and pure chance. Now, here we were, eating ice cream in her kitchen, her little sister singing more loudly than she needed to and finger painting on paper that the paint would clearly bleed through, with her father looking at me like I was after his older daughter's innocence. Anika poked fun at me, kept me up at night asking me questions, and drove me absolutely nuts during the day.

And I'd never been happier.

77527583R00109

Made in the USA
Columbia, SC
22 September 2017